Bullet Points
Volume 3

BULLET POINTS
VOLUME 3

Nathan W. Toronto

Editor

BULLET POINT PRESS

an imprint of
TORONTO INTERNATIONAL MEDIA

This anthology is entirely a work of fiction. The names, characters, and incidents portrayed in it are the product of the authors' imaginations. Any resemblance to actual persons, living or dead, or events or localities is entirely coincidental.

Paperback edition, first impression, July 15, 2023
ISBN 979-8-9873933-3-8

The Arabic block *noon* colophon is a trademark of Bullet Point Press.

Cover design by Nathan W. Toronto. Cover © 2023 Nathan W. Toronto. Cover image by Liu Zishan (used under license). Interior design by Nathan W. Toronto using the Spectral LaTeX font.

Other editions: ISBN 979-8-9873933-4-5 (electronic)

To those who fight and die,
And to those who live on,
May we fight for you as you have for us.
—N. T.

Read *Bullet Points*, volume 1, with stories from H. G. Wells, David Drake, James C. Glass, Tony Ballantyne, Walter Jon Williams, Nathan W. Toronto, and others.

Preface: The Levels of War

SCHOLARS DEBATE THE LEVELS of war—how many there are, and whether tactical, operational, and strategic covers it. My view is that there are only two: that at which war is personal, violent, and visceral; and that at which it is possible to reduce human lives and experiences to distant numbers or dispassionate plans. A fair amount of military science fiction focuses on the first, personal level, but the tension in perspective between these two levels can help us make sense of the avoidable insanity that is war.

I choose stories for *Bullet Points* because I love them, but also to reflect on war and warfare from both a personal and a distant perspective. While war is an entrenched human institution, using science fiction to reimagine the experience is a useful way to bridge the gap between those who fight and those who don't. I actively seek out authors with military experience, and I reject a lot of very well-written stories because the authors demonstrate a profound ignorance for how the military works and how military members think. *Bullet Points* is not a place for anti-war screeds that catalog the litany of evils that war offers.

Rather, *Bullet Points* recognizes that war is complex and that it harbors both evil and virtue. War requires sacrifice for the greater good and warfare breeds endurance and camaraderie in ways that other human endeavors do not. As a society, we outsource the management of violence to those who fight, often without recognizing what that entails, blissfully unaware of the burden we lay at their feet. Even after war ends and warfare has abated, the effects of that experience on those who fight often endure for years, if not decades. *Bullet Points* helps the reader come to terms with this complexity.

If the stories in this anthology make the reader feel a bit uncomfortable, good. We owe it to ourselves to look war in the face and stare down its cruelty and its hope, its better angels and its tragedy. The stories in this anthology are organized from most personal and visceral to most distant and dispassionate in perspective. In all cases, however, these stories invite readers to ponder war and warfare at all levels, regardless of how many there may be.

—Nathan W. Toronto, ed.

Read *Bullet Points*, volume 2, with stories from Joe Haldeman, Jenna Hanchey, Eric Fomley, Tabitha Lord, Ian R. MacLeod, Rich Larson, Shannon Fay, Pedro Iniguez, and others.

CONTENTS

1 Forget Me Not   1
MIA DALIA

2 Used Armor Smell   4
A. P. HOWELL

3 Hounds   7
J. T. GILL

4 Inversion Point   15
LISA SHORT

5 Bone and Acid and Rushing Waves   21
ADDISON SMITH

6 Something Else   23
CONRAD GARDNER

7 And Kill Them   27
WILLIAM R. D. WOOD

8 Closing Time   29
T. M. THOMAS

9 The Golden Rays of the Morning Sun   31
MARC A. CRILEY

10 The Thin Rising Line   39
KIRAN KAUR SAINI

11 Merry-Go-Round   42
LIAM HOGAN

12 Artist Known   45
CAIAS WARD

13 Spun Yarn   47
RAY DALEY

14 The Compulsion of Venus   52
C. B. DROEGE

15 We'll Make Them Pay   55
DANIEL CROW

16 Ships Made of Guns   58
M. V. MELCER

17 War Around the Clock   60
LARRY HODGES

18 The Phantom Tolbukhin   63
HARRY TURTLEDOVE

19 The Battle of Dorking   71
GEORGE TOMKYNS CHESNEY

Forget Me Not

Mia Dalia

There is no more personal experience than the long memory of war, as this story from Mia Dalia shows. Dalia is an internationally published author, a lifelong reader, and a longtime reviewer of all things fantastic, thrilling, scary, and strange. Her short fiction has been published online by *Night Terror Novels*, *50-Word Stories*, *Flash Fiction Magazine*, *Pyre Magazine*, *Tales from the Moonlit Path*, and in print anthologies by Sunbury Press, HellBound Press, and Black Ink Fiction, among others. Her fiction will be featured in upcoming anthologies from Wandering Wave Press, Off-Topic Publishing, and Psycho Toxin Press. Her debut novelette, *Smile So Red*, was recently released to rave reviews. The next novelette, *The Trunk*, followed suit shortly after. Her debut novel, *Estate Sale*, came out in 2023. "Forget Me Not" is original to *Bullet Points*.

THE NIGHT CLOSED IN on him. The sound of artillery had at some point became a background drone like the white noise machine he used to fall asleep to. But every so often, a bullet whizzed by in a close call, and it still jarred him. He was amazed something still had the power to jar him—he'd become so desensitized by the last few months.

COULDN'T REMEMBER THE LAST time he showered; his feet were a mess of bloody blisters, there somehow was never quite enough food or time to eat. And sleep…he still slept but it was so far from restful that it seemed it ought to have a different word to describe it altogether.

These people—they spoke his language. He was shooting at people who spoke his mother's tongue, and it felt profoundly wrong. None of it seemed real. From the day it began.

This wasn't a war his grandfather told him stories about. This was ... something else entirely.

And he was here because he was told to be here. There'd never been a choice, not really. A third-generation military man; it was in his blood, in his bones. He'd never even entertained the idea of doing anything else with his life.

It was hot, too hot, and humid too. Sweat pouring down his face occasionally made it through the long thick lashes he used to get teased about and into his eyes—it stung. He wiped his dirty forehead with the dusty sleeve of his uniform. Took a moment to orient himself.

Where were they? Oh, yes. He remembered now. A place so small it barely made it onto most maps, but strategically significant enough to attack.

They didn't want an all-out battle, but the locals seemed ready for them. Armed with anything from handguns to pitchforks—*pitchforks*; steel glint of determination in their eyes. These people would fight to the death to protect what was theirs.

From what he saw earlier during the day, there wasn't much to protect here. The village (*selo*) appeared to have been stuck in time as if the pervasive modern world seldom dared to find its way in. The place was positively medieval in a way. You could easily imagine these ancient-looking houses as *dvoryshche* homesteads, self-sufficient and family-owned and -operated.

He loved history, studied it extensively, still read heavy nonfiction tomes on it whenever he got a chance. Maybe he should have been a historian instead.

The village must have been hit by the collectivization efforts once. The old machine-tractor stations stood abandoned on the outskirts—modernization attempts summarily rejected by the locals, who went back to agriculture in their own way, tried-and-true methods that had with-

stood the test of time.

He didn't want to fight these people, didn't want to kill these people. He hoped they could be persuaded to lay down their weapons and disperse. But it was all too far gone by now; the diplomacy attempts over before they even began.

It no longer mattered who shot first. The second the bullet struck a ten-year-old girl—he could still remember the doll she had in her hand, not the girl herself, but the doll. The *motanka* doll—a peculiar local toy, made of fabric and left faceless as if open to the imagination's own projections. The one the girl held was clad in a colorful dress, white and red, with black and green accents. More red added as the girl's blood splattered on it and then all dust as it hit the ground.

He thought the image of that doll would haunt him for the rest of his days.

The girl's death marked the moment the conflict turned into a battle and then, all too soon, a slaughter. The soldiers saw their own blood; saw red and went mad. There was no stopping them. The brutality they visited upon that village felt medieval too. Primal in the worst way—the giving-in to one's basest instincts. It reeked of blood; he could taste it like the copper of old coins. The smell of death was everywhere. Too terrible to describe, it permeated his skin, his bones; he didn't think he'd ever get rid of it. Perhaps it would follow him everywhere, this olfactory representation of his sins. And he would never be free.

In the end, there was fire. To obliterate the very memory of the place—and their actions in it—from existence.

H E SNAPPED INTO REALITY at her touch. The nightmare faded away, like it always did, clinging to the peripherals, but no longer pulling focus.

They were parked near a wheat field as wide as the eye could see. It smelled fresh, calm, happy.

The wind stirred the stalks gently. It looked like a dance.

Nina looked up at him and squeezed his hand. "Where'd you go just now?"

"Nowhere," he shook his head. "I'm here."

She looked beautiful in her red summer dress, her long hair, pulled back on weekdays into a professionally slick ponytail, now free-flowing down her shoulders. Eyes as blue as the cloudless sky above them. Love of his life. Funny the turns life takes to bring you to where you're meant to be.

"Wanna walk around?"

There were paths, dirt stumped into submission by who knows how many feet over who knows how long. It was quiet. Peaceful.

"I used to love it here a lifetime ago," Nina said wistfully.

"What was it then?" The place seemed so familiar somehow.

"A village," she said. "A village that vanished."

He felt himself bleed before he felt the blade— it must've been that sharp. He dropped to his knees looking up at her, questions in his eyes. "Wh..."

"You were there. I remember you. I remember everything and I won't stop until I bring you all back."

The blade moved again, and he fell at her feet. The last thing he saw was her face turn featureless against the perfect summer sky.

Used Armor Smell

A. P. HOWELL

A. P. Howell's jobs have spanned the alphabet from archivist to webmaster. She lives with her husband, their two kids, and a pair of energetic pups. Her short fiction has appeared in a variety of magazines and anthologies, including *Daily Science Fiction, Martian: The Magazine of Science Fiction Drabbles, Underland Arcana, Translunar Travelers Lounge,* and *In Somnio: A Collection of Modern Gothic Horror.* Her work has been nominated for the Pushcart Prize and Honorably Mentioned in Ellen Datlow's *The Best Horror of the Year Volume Thirteen.* "Used Armor Smell" was nominated for the Brave New Weird Award and Honorably Mentioned in Alex Woodroe's *Brave New Weird: The Best New Weird Horror 2022* (Tenebrous Press). "Used Armor Smell," which explores the connection between combat and gender, originally appeared in *Dread Space* (Shacklebound Books).

J ANOT'S ARMOR NO LONGER had that new-armor smell.

NEW-ARMOR SMELL WAS different from new-suit smell; was different from new-car smell and new-carpet smell. But all of those scents pinged something in the human brain, created a sense of purity. Said *this* was a new thing, recently created by complex industrial processes, but untouched by human hands. (Except technicians and installers and salespeople and logistics specialists and—it was always rumored, no matter what the usage hours buried in HUD settings claimed—an unlucky previous owner who'd hemorrhaged all over the interior.) The newness smelled of ownership, mastery, and exclusive rights.

The new-armor smell had faded, replaced by Janot's own smell. Usually, it was undetectable. The armor did an excellent job of wicking away sweat and cycling the air (it still smelled like recycled air, but Janot couldn't recall the last time e'd inhaled unmediated atmosphere). The armor's plumbing was mated to Janot's—no diapers, no drips, no offensive odors—and sometimes e missed the catheter while walking down a corridor to the toilet.

The armor was even good about cleaning vomit. Janot could smell it, however, and there were still bits splattered on eir faceplate, visible behind the urgent reds of the HUD. E could also smell the coppery scent of blood.

Couldn't feel the arm at all, not since the whiteout pain of . . . seconds earlier? When shit happened, it happened fast. The HUD reported painkillers and stimulants and tourniquet protocols: bright bullet points that could be easily dismissed, distractions from survival. Janot tried to flex eir fingers and the gauntlet flexed in response.

Did e even have those fingers any more, or was the gauntlet just filled with red jelly, reacting to nervous impulses sent to a limb that no longer existed?

Beyond the HUD, beyond the faceplate, the world was dark and full of smoke and fire. Weapons fire, bright traceries crossing the sky to their terminus, and the orange-red evidence of atmospheric O_2. Janot could only see eir unit with the HUD, and it showed fewer points of light than e liked. The enemy was completely invisible.

The armor's systems gave Janot an instant's warning before the igneous rock formation at eir back split and exploded outward. Time enough to lunge away, flattened to the ground. The new wave of red warnings indicated blunt force impacts, nothing to compromise the armor.

Janot tried to move. The arm e could feel and the arm e couldn't both moved, no sign of exacerbated injury. One leg fine, one pinned under a hunk of rock that had melted along some of its surfaces and was hot enough there to do some minor damage to the armor. The angle was awkward but e rose to eir knees, arms and back pushing against the weight on eir calf and foot. It shifted— Janot felt it in the changing angle and saw it in the HUD, couldn't feel it in the leg; it had either been protected by the armor or the pain masked by the meds. Janot wanted to check, but navi-

gating the HUD's menus seemed too complex a task.

Not a good sign. The sounds echoing in eir ears—not quite ringing, not quite a whine— clearly originated in Janot's own skull.

Also a bad sign.

E was on eir feet, rifle grasped in both gauntlets, moving toward a highlighted position on the HUD's map. Not a decision Janot had made, not a movement e had made. E cycled through readouts, almost at random, saw the spike in the armor's processing. It was running very expensive calculations. The situational awareness built over the course of human evolution was difficult to replicate computationally, even with the expert training dumped into expert systems.

A painfully bright point lit up the HUD. The rifle snapped up. Janot registered the recoil, deadened by the armor, and then the disappearance of the bright point. E looked past the display, a reflex despite knowing the target wouldn't be visible. Oily black smoke boiled in the air, but Janot's attention was caught by the red speckling on the inside of the faceplate. Eir next exhalation added more.

E moved through the smoke, rifle ready to engage. That processing flare was back and growing stronger, the armor making decisions Janot couldn't. (Wouldn't? But no, the armor was doing what it was supposed to do—what e was supposed to do—moving toward the objective glowing on the map.)

E tried to feel the good arm, the good leg, the pinned leg, finally whatever was left of the bad arm. The way the skinsuit snagged against the armor when e lifted a leg, the pressure just above the knee, the place e tapped eir thumbnail against the gauntlet . . . nothing. Janot dug through menus in search of medical readouts. Was the system burying them so e wouldn't be distracted? Not that it mattered. E couldn't get a medevac in the middle of a firefight. The system was doing what it could, the processing graph burning into Janot's retinas.

Another flare on the map and the armor took the shot. This time, something returned fire and pressure blossomed across Janot's ribs. The armor took a second shot and the enemy disappeared from the HUD.

Janot could barely see that detail. The world beyond the faceplate blurred—some of that seemed like motion, the armor bearing em implacably forward, but Janot couldn't tell for sure, eir sense of balance perhaps damaged with eir hearing. E tried to say something, even though there was no one to listen. E tasted more blood.

Janot couldn't smell recycled air any more, or even vomit, only the smell of blood. The smell of emself, of desperation and hopelessness.

Hounds

J. T. GILL

"Hounds" is an original *Bullet Points* story that screams for the reader to understand, in some small way, what war does to a family. J. T. Gill's work has appeared in *Daily Science Fiction*, *Perihelion Science Fiction*, and *The Molotov Cocktail*, where he won the 2015 Flash Fool Contest. This is a story that sticks with the reader long after the pages have stopped turning.

CARLISLE—THE HULKING GUARD from D Wing—wakes me with a grunt and a nudge. "Warden needs you," he rumbles, his black form shifting in the darkness.

I DRESS IN THE dark, Carlisle's silhouette at the door, arms crossed. My optic reads 3:42 AM, which narrows the realm of possibilities as to what this is about…though I have a guess.

We march down the hallway, fluorescents sizzling overhead. The monitor at the end of the hall is offline—flaccid, pointing at the floor. Rehabilitation centers are low on the current System Administrator's list of priorities. Over the past three years, Chamberlain Rehab Center's budget has been slashed four times, and between the lights and the security, you can almost hear the money escaping. There's even a rumor going around some inmates might be released altogether, their sentences commuted, though I find that hard to believe.

The courtyard shines like a sungun. It's snowing, big flakes drifting through the whitelight orbs. Shivering, I zip my cryocloak to the neck as we head for the administration building…but Carlisle surprises me, pivoting towards D Wing instead. I jog to keep up.

"Thought the Warden wanted to see me," I say.

Carlisle grunts, a cloud of steam billowing around his face.

I hadn't much interaction with any of the guards, least of all Carlisle, but I know two things: the Warden likes him, and he has a penchant for *emphatic* rehabilitation. It's not my department, but I've seen one or two inmates leave D Wing in medpods, usually with blood caked to their skulls.

Inside, the wing is silent. Our footsteps echo on the smartfloor, lightprints rippling in our wake. The cell blocks are split in six directions. A central hub with narrow brick and glass canyon spokes.

The lights are all on, and the cells are transparent, most of the inmates in bed, their neon jumpsuits like garish paint stains. Each one's colors coded based on the severity of their crimes. Red are severe, life sentences and death row. Orange is more moderate. Armed robbery, hit and run. Ten to thirty years.

D Wing is mostly reds.

The Warden is pacing at the end of the fourth spoke, her heels jabbing the floor. Even at four in the morning, she's dressed in a smart pencil skirt and gray blazer, her hair wrenched back in a chopsticks-skewered bun. A couple of Administrator officials stand by, one young, one old, staring into space while they check their optics. As we approach, their gazes sharpen, the milky glaze fading from their pupils.

"Paulson," the Warden says.

"Yes, ma'am."

"Are your Hounds ready?"

"What's the situation?"

She nods to Carlisle. *Explain.*

Carlisle juts his chin to the cell block adjacent us. "Prisoner 392 escaped sometime between nightly check-in and midnight patrol."

I wait, thinking he might want to add some color. Like maybe who Prisoner 392 was, or what he was in for … but Carlisle confirms what I already know: he's not one for words.

I gaze in, enjoying the smell of Lysol and limes. Their eyes are on me.

The job is easy. The Hounds will hunt him down within an hour, hardly worth my time.

Unless there's something special about this one. Besides, I don't get chances like this often. I can't help myself.

"So?" I say.

Carlisle stiffens, but the Warden's hand goes up like a portcullis.

"I've heard rumors we're losing our funding," I say. "An escaped inmate seems like an easy way to cut costs." I grin. "Unless this one's special."

This time it's one of the suits who speaks up. The old one. Broken spider web wisps of hair cling to his scalp.

"I wouldn't impute motives on the Administrator's office," he says, chewing chapped lips.

I keep my eyes on the warden. She can't say why I'm really here, not in front of these men, but we both know.

"Every inmate in this rehabilitation center represents an investment," she says. "An *opportunity*." I catch the shimmer in her eye as she steps closer.

"Yes, ma'am," I say.

I WAS SITTING ON the edge of my front porch when the mech officer came up the lane, rolling through the gravel on bipedal treads. I knew what was coming, but I forced myself to sit there and listen to every word of that pre-recorded message so many heard that day: your son has been killed in service of his country.

I asked what happened. An ambush on Junger. The Massacre.

The memory stings like the wind as I trudge past the recreation fields.

We keep the Hounds in a locked shed out here, beyond the grounds and the whitelights of the main courtyard. Away from the warmth. Even in the folds of my cryocloak, the wind's kisses are like those of an unwanted ex. I focus on what I can control. *Tracks. Exposure.* Somewhere out there 392 is slowing down.

The shed is a momentary relief from the cold. Inside, the Hounds are clamped in their charging stations—spindly mech legs curled up and over their central nervous systems like dead spiders. I go down the line, punching the upboot for each. Photoreceptors come to life, strobing piss yellow as their servo motors sputter into action, grinding against the cold.

Dolly, Denver … and Duke.

Signal lights slide to blue as they connect to the network. Carlisle uploaded temporary access to 392's file. I open it through my optic.

Inmate data floods the system, everything we have on 392. Injections, blood types, medication, preferences, criminal history. I tab the surveillance footage and check the vids.

He's tall, lanky. Tattoos etched up the back of his neck, right arm replaced with a pneumatic claw. Red jumpsuit when he enters for nightly check-in. Nothing out of place...and then the feed goes dark.

I gnaw the inside of my cheek. As much as I'd like to believe this an oddity, it's not. Feeds go dark. Blame it on the budget cuts. If prisoners knew how often it happened, we'd have trouble preventing everyone from attempting to escape.

The Hounds send out a signal, a single synchronous bark. Duke bumps against his restraint clamp. I strap a pair of tracking goggles over my head, slip the detonator in the pocket of my cryocloak, and hop on the speedcycle at the back of the shed.

"All right," I say. "Let's go catch this... *opportunity.*"

I key open the door and release their clamps. The four of us tear out into the snow.

WATCHING A HOUND MOVE is like watching a demon. They're fast and gangling and move in a kind of fluid treachery, servo motors whining, legs snickering together when in full gallop.

At top speed, I've tracked them at 65 kph, but that's when they've locked a signal.

All inmates are given a tracking injection upon arrival. It enters the bloodstream and cycles into permanent stasis, barring a blood transfusion. I've only seen one escapee get beyond the grounds, and that was before the Hound program came to Chamberlain, back when Carlisle and his cronies oversaw prisoner recapture.

That particular inmate avoided the search team for 17 hours. They couldn't match his signal—just kept circling before they stumbled on him passed out against a tree in a pool of his own blood, a sharpened stick protruding from his wrist.

So there really is no way of getting the injection out without killing yourself.

The Hounds fan out. I stick with Denver, running scans as we barrel through the cold, searching for a lock. His range is limited due to the snow, but a momentary break in the clouds gives him something.

My optic chimes as crosshairs fall, screwing down over the signal.

A few klicks west.

Denver barks, rearing back on his single hind leg before he bolts, galloping between the trees, throwing up white clouds in his wake. Duke and Dolly slide in on either side, the three of them forming a triangle, tearing through the woods with electrifying intensity.

I'd love to admire them run, but I figure it can't hurt to redeem the time reviewing 392's file instead.

The entry picture is a mug of his drab face. Pale and sunken. The tattoo is invisible from the front, but along the back you can see it's a dog, staring with baleful eyes and droopy ears.

It's a bit of a sob story, his file. Ex-military, which is sad, because there's no fixing army brats. They get out, flinching and flexing with their PTSD and concussion history and soon they come riding our way, clamps circling their wrists and baleful eyes of their own.

He's been in for seven years, which is more than long enough, except he saw combat. Front lines. Boots on the ground for the Dahlia Invasion, and...

And then I stop, because this guy was stationed on Junger...The Massacre.

I swallow, and tab the realclip from his helmcam.

Women, children fleeing while he pants, turning one way, then the other. Someone falls in front of him, sloshing through a plum-colored puddle. An enormous plume of orange and white blooms in the distance.

I turn it off when a chainsaw starts to grind.

It was a month before I ventured outside the house, after the news. I had realclips of my little boy, a stock of brandy in the basement, and the same detonator I keep in my pocket now. Those were dark nights … and then … like an extended hand, an opportunity from Chamberlain Rehabilitation Center, and a way out. A way back into the world.

My world erupts in a thundercrack and everything falls into slow motion as my vision doubles.

My optic autocloses the file, the HUD kicking into action. Dolly disappears in an enormous mushroom cloud to my left. I hear the final shriek of metal pulping her to bits before one of her front legs, sheared off at the calf, flies from the cloud. End over end, it collides with the front of my cycle, splintering the forward repulsor.

A queasy feeling in the pit of my stomach as I go over the handlebars and then everything is silent and there's only optics. Sky. Trees. Snow.

The world goes dark.

THE SIGNAL WAS WEAK, *but there. Like finding the heartbeat on an ultrasound. Connected to the maindrive, I could communicate with him—blips of encrypted green scrolling in the black. Hours in the shed, that final line of text like a ray of sun: What about you?*

My cryocloak's shot. First thing through my head. Like a boot plunged shin-deep in icy water, the cold seeps in from every direction at once. First, it's numbing, then torturous. My ears ring a single note refrain.

Flakes are raining from the trees in powdery clouds. My nostrils flare with the smell of burnt metal.

I try to move my arms and legs, but I'm half buried. My optic's glitching, which is a concussion indicator. Blinking, I wriggle free. Duke and Denver hold position a few meters off, waiting

for orders. They're grouped around a blackened hole in the snow, smoke streaming from it like a just-erupted volcano. Scattered flaming tongues flicker around the perimeter.

Dolly.

The shipment came in late, the delivery truck hacking as it downshifted through the dropgate. They dropped her on the pavement behind the service entrance, curled in stasis like a dead spider. I wasn't impressed. But when it started to rain, the drops tinkling her metal frame, she blinked to life.

I kneel beside Duke and Denver, staring down into the crater.

Amidst the shards of ash and metal, a single photoreceptor gazes back up at us, glowing blue. I shiver, trying not to think about the kind of trauma she felt. The central housing's well protected, but nothing can save you from that kind of blast.

Duke and Denver connect to my optic. They're running coms, scanning the area. I'm sure Carlisle and whoever else is doing the same.

As if summoned, Carlisle appears, a holo spirit in the smoke.

"We lost your feed," he says.

"I lost one of the Hounds," I say, trying to keep my voice steady. "Looks like a bomb."

His reflection warbles, splicing. "You still have the other two. Find him," he says, and his face drifts, leaving me, Duke, and Denver alone in the woods.

BASED ON THE BLAST radius, this wasn't a home protection civilian mine. The fire's still burning steady when I finally find the cycle, buried in a drift thirty meters from the crater.

It's trashed. Not worth patching. Which leaves me with two options: I can walk, or I can ride with one of the Hounds.

My optic's still glitching, playing warped images across my field of view. From what I can tell, the signal's farther now.

I opt for the Hounds, climbing aboard Denver. His onboard engine is like a heat stove.

We're limited, with me on his back, so while Denver and I canter along, Duke blazes back off, driven by that singular focus he's always had.

*T*HE WHIR OF ENGINE *parts as he comes alive. The new leg scrabbles, twitches, and then he's up, hulking high like the bots they pit against humans in the underground. That might have been the miracle…and then came those scrolling lines of code.*

The ad read: "Lab technician. Competitive pay + benefits. Interact with the machinery responsible for protecting the attendees."

Sitting across the table from the Warden, my face clean-shaven for the first-time in weeks. She offered me the job on the spot. I started the next day, and as promised, they brought me Duke. He was missing a leg, but otherwise in good condition.

I worked on him for two weeks before we spoke. A new leg shipped in from Vankirk. Photoreceptors from Busteen. A little at a time. Long days spent in the shed, tinkering on the central nervous system, watching how-to videos, eager and anxious.

And then of course came Dolly and Denver.

I was the one who was there when Duke walked for the first time. I saw when Dolly perked, suddenly aware of the prisoners' signals in the yard. And when Denver stepped in front of an inmate who tried to rush me in the rec yard, a shiv up his sleeve.

That's why I stayed. It was for them.

*M*Y OPTIC IS GLITCHING again when Duke goes dark, but even with the signal break a hollow feeling opens in the pit of my stomach.

Denver senses it too, pulling up short, as if listening.

For a moment it's utterly quiet, the world shrouded in a white blanket.

And then Denver is off and running, out into the open, and we see a pillar of smoke rising in the distance.

I can't speak, can't move. I'm losing my boy all over again. It's the same as Dolly, ash and snow falling back to earth down in the valley below. I get that same sick just-erupted volcano feeling again, and when Denver bolts all I can do is cling on, numb fingers digging into warm metal. Between his jolting and the glitch in my optic, it's hard to determine exactly how far he is, but moving this fast I know it won't matter.

Duke's nowhere to be seen. The crater's dead center of a clearing this time, smoke billowing into the sky, inky thick with altitude.

My optic spasms, hard enough to make me wince. But when it clears and Duke's signal appears on the map again, he isn't anywhere near us.

He's nearly five klicks away, and I breathe a sigh of relief.

Of hope.

A flicker of movement to my right.

I turn. Not fast enough. 392's pneumatic claw connects with the side of my skull like a wrecker. Pain ripples down my right side. My optic blares static. Something sticky and warm in my eyes as I hit the ground. A wet shard feeling of snow pressed against my face.

Somehow, I'm still conscious. Denver is spidertromping through the snow, lurching over me with scissor-snickering limbs. I push myself up onto all fours and my vision tunnels into blackness…but I breathe, force myself back awake.

Inmate 392 is a blur of speed as he spins, shimmies, ducks everything Denver sends at him. Denver's every movement should kill him, slice him in half. His mandibles clip the air, snapping like pinchers. Legs whickering in deadly arcs.

But 392's a phantom. It's like watching a choreographed dance, snow spitting, spinning in every direction, that pneumatic claw pistoning, working, whining.

I'm watching, not comprehending much besides movement, pushing myself backward, away from the combat.

I make it to a tree, and things start to make more sense as my vision returns. Denver chirruping behind me. Optic back online. Carlisle in my face.

"What's happening?"

I close him out and send a ping to Duke, hear the chime in my head as he responds. Slumping down against the tree, I grab handfuls of snow and pack them against the side of my throbbing, sodden head. In my wake, a blood-stained trail, bright as a Chamberlain jumpsuit.

It's sad, watching how it all unfolds. 392's like a dancing boxer, breaking in and out, hammering blows with that claw. Punching through a leg, denting his carapace.

If he can hold out for Duke, though. He'll be here in seconds, and quick as 392 may be, he's no match for the two of them at once.

It's as if 392 has heard me thinking. He slips one arm between Denver's legs, reaching for the photoreceptor.

The sound of my own breathing as Duke approaches on the optic. I should be doing something. I should be helping. My head throbs.

And that's when I hear it.

Denver keens, and it's like no sound I've heard before. I whip my head around and watch as 392 bares his teeth. He's gotten his arm inside, gotten hold of something deep.

I push myself up against the tree, yelling.

A wrenching sound. The shrieking scream of metal on metal as 392 pulls away, teeth barred.

Denver's photoreceptor comes with it, the pulsing eye on the end and what looks like a squid of wires mixed with a pulpy, bloody mass.

Denver's brain.

I watch in horror as the light drains from his photoreceptor, and then I'm up, staggering forward, but I can feel the blood rushing to my head, and I hardly see when 392 tosses Denver's remains aside with a chuff.

392's mouth moves. He's saying something—I can't make out the words, but he only makes it about halfway across the clearing because Duke has arrived.

And Duke is the best—always has been.

Duke roars—a bullhorn scree that rattles the trees and then cliffdrops silent.

392 braces, but only just, and even then it's like watching someone brace against a freighter. Duke rams him like a plow, mashing him into the snow, legs stabbing, hammering him into the ground.

I stagger back to my feet, and for the third time Carlisle's in my face coming through in a signal now bright as day.

"Paulson. Report."

"Not now," I say, but when I try to close him out, he only drifts up into the top right-hand corner of my optic.

392 is sitting in the snow, Duke towering over him, one leg raised, poised like a cocked javelin, a scorpion stinger.

"You're coming back with us," I manage, and the effort of speech is like dragging a dagger through my windpipe. The cold shreds every word.

He rolls onto his back, his body battered, his chest expanding and deflating silently. He keeps one eye on me.

"Well done," the Warden says, her voice placid.

They're watching my feed. They have my eyes.

A rumble above us. Snow blows, rippling around my cryocloak.

I look up. A Crab—the center's lone transport—hovers right above us. Duke just stands there, the flakes pinging off him like bullets.

The Crab lowers into the clearing, water running off the stabilizers. A creak as the loading bay yawns open and the repulsors power down to twin blue jets.

Carlisle's framed in the opening, the "C" on his Chamberlain uniform polished to a sheen.

He struts down the ramp. "I'll take it from here," he says, peering down at 392, and then nods to Duke, who wraps the prisoner at the feet and hauls him to the Crab's cargo hold. I can see a medpod sitting inside like a white coffin.

"Wait," I say, and trigger my override, ordering a hold on Duke. He stops at the bay door.

Carlisle takes another two steps before he realizes Duke's halted. He turns, and he knows it's me because I see his jaw set like a pneumatic limb.

Then the Warden appears before me—a little ghost among the trees.

"Carlisle," she says. "Let me handle this."

"Duke stays with me," I say.

From kilometers away, she unplugs my optic. I'm blind.

⬛

*D*UKE WAS THE FIRST, *and the only reason I took the job at Chamberlain. As promised, his file dropped on my desk a day after the machinery arrived in a wood plank box with HOUND stenciled on the outside in military black. A bomb squad bot. A three-legged dog.*

The file was everything—the history, just like countless others I'd read at Chamberlain. Ex-military. Razor Taser cut him in half during an ambush on Junger. The Massacre. Nearly nothing left. There was no medpod—and I remember averting my gaze at those realclips, the smell of cauterized, charred flesh coming off the image like smoke.

And what was left after they harvested?

His brain. Sealed in lifewrap and shipped back to the barracks where they repurposed with spare parts and an adapter. A kid from Southie, a living scarecrow.

My son. Now a Hound.

So of course I took the job at Chamberlain. Those dark days and long nights with only a bottle of brandy and the detonator for comfort... and then hope. I could see my boy again. Maybe not in the way I had hoped, but this was a gift. An opportunity.

Denver was next—the gunner from Zinc who bathed in napalm torching a nest of Ozarks, and Dolly after that. A Squad Chief near the Baltic, obliterated by friendly fire when her own troops panicked in a smokefield.

We spent those nights in the shed, the four of us, talking through the maindrive once I hooked them up, my optic running translations.

Their memories had been wiped. Call signs instead of names, rage instead of families. Unattached, unfeeling... but still human, their death experiences intact... and one of them was my son.

What came through were singular sights and sounds. Images which didn't make sense through the computer. Duke told me about when he died, how he felt the warmth go first.

I would stare at the machine on the ground in front of me, blowing on my hands, flurries slithering under the doorframe while lines of chat filtered across the screen... and for a while I forgot about the detonator I had kept so close for so long.

The Warden approved. When I had the three of them up online, she came by, asking to take a look.

"This is what Chamberlain is," she said, smiling inside the shed, the three of them wired into their charging stations. "A chance for change. Opportunity."

I nodded, a frozen tear notching my cheek.

"Maybe you can lose the grief in your pocket," she added, and smiled at my look of surprise.

⬛

*I*T'S AS IF MY *eyes have been removed, the darkness is so complete. I can feel the cold whirling, hear Carlisle striding up into the loading bay. The clang of Duke's legs behind him.

"Take me offline," the Warden says, and I hear the little static click as the recording disconnects.

"The bombs," I say, trying to understand, craving resolution.

"We triggered Dolly's self-destruct. She asked for it before you left. We had to wait until you were off-grounds so it was out-of-network. Untraceable. Carlisle triggered the second explosion from the Crab. We needed a diversion to keep your boy away."

I'm stunned, unable to speak.

"They asked for self-destruct," she says, almost defensively. "You saw how easily Denver gave up."

In my mind, I see 392 ripping Denver's photoreceptor free, a squid of wires attached to a bloody mass.

Inside the Crab, I can hear the medpod slide open, Carlisle grunting as he lifts the prisoner's body inside.

"I want you to know the program was real, Paulson," The Warden says. Chagrin in her voice. "The Administrator's officers gave me orders this morning to discontinue. They decided it wasn't worth the effort, giving unwilling subjects a second chance. Then she drops the bomb on me. "But they want Duke repurposed. Shipped back out to the front lines. He's too good to waste."

I can't move. Can't speak. Did I do this? Alone in the shed with lines of code blinking across the screen…how many times did they ask to be set free? And I ignored them. Consumed in my own grief. Even my own son, trapped behind my manual override and denial. Fear of loss outweighed my love for him.

"Maybe it's a good thing you kept the grief in your pocket," she says.

I think of Duke, trapped inside the carapace up there, a hound with no heart, and Carlisle, and then I realize what the Warden's just said.

In your pocket.

My detonator.

"Carlisle!" I shout, thumbing the switch inside my cryocloak.

A chuckle, but I hear his boots on the bay door, tromping out from behind the medpod.

"I never—" he begins, and that's all I need to know where he's standing.

"I love you, son!" I call.

And then I throw the detonator as hard as I can in their direction.

The explosion blooms like a dying sun, collapsing in on itself and then slinging everything outward. Heat bakes my face, a welcome warmth amidst the cold until a stray shard of metal flies free and punctures my stomach like a pike. The air whooshes out of my lungs. My knees hit the snow, ears ringing.

And then a terrible thought enters my brain, which will be sealed in lifewrap and repurposed in some barracks with spare parts and an adapter.

Where will I wake up?

I wonder, and wait for the warmth to go first.

Inversion Point

Lisa Short

Lisa Short is a Texas-born, Kansas-bred writer of fantasy, science fiction, and horror. She has an honorable discharge from the United States Army, a degree in chemical engineering, and twenty years' experience as a professional engineer. Lisa currently lives in Maryland with her husband, youngest child, father-in-law, and cats. She is a member of the Science Fiction & Fantasy Writers Association, Horror Writers Association, and Codex Writers. "Inversion Point" is original to *Bullet Points*, and is a reminder that in war everything is simple, but the simplest thing is difficult.

THE AIRLOCK SEAL THUDDED home barely a meter above Amelie's head. The echo shot pain through her ears. She cradled her aching temples in gloved hands and scrunched up her face, free at last from Tech Sergeant Pravin's sharply observant glare.

SHE HAD BARELY MADE it into formation before the third watch bell had sounded—she had looked like death warmed over in the brief glimpse that was all she'd dared to take of her face before sprinting out of the section dormitory to Auxiliary Engineering. She wouldn't have been surprised if Pravin had made a note of it before he handed out the watch assignments.

And then probably changed hers, mid-stream—*where is the* worst *place I can put a specialist with a terminal hangover?* Amelie imagined his evil grin—*that won't endanger the ship no matter* how *fucked up she is on watch.* That thought was less palatable; Amelie was aware that showing up on duty in a less-than-stellar physical and mental state was not the way to leave the best of impressions on her superiors.

And it wasn't true anyway—she absolutely

could endanger the ship from here. The Auxiliary Engineering maintenance tube ran along the ship's belly, all the way from stem to stern, giving it not just virtual but also direct physical access to all critical ship's systems. Other than the Main Engineering bay itself, Amelie couldn't think of any place where someone could potentially do *more* damage to the ship. Though that damage would have to be intentional; mere incompetence could be foiled easily enough by the maintenance tube's own fail-safes. But—*message received,* Amelie thought dismally. Though she supposed she deserved it, especially right before inversion point…

Two years.

Two years aboard as the ship sailed blindly through irrational space, the mathematical fantasy that allowed ships to sidestep the relentless weight of light years separating Earth's solar system from all the colonies, some so distant Amelie had never even seen their stars from her own night sky.

Never so much as a toe off the ship…

She could handle it—all her psych evaluations said so. Command would never risk one of their unimaginably expensive interstellar ships in the hands of someone with tendencies that might trigger some deadly chain of events in the lightless, soundless depths of irrational space. She *could* handle it. She could.

But the captain's address over ship's comm the night before told them that they'd nearly reached inversion point. And that was when Amelie had started downing not just that week's, but next week's alcohol rations too, mindlessly, one after the other. For all she knew, she'd drunk all next month's to boot, and who knew what else—*she* certainly couldn't remember…

And now here she was, Amelie's wristcom beeped irritably at her. She'd stood on the tube ladder motionless for far too long, a good ten minutes at least. Doing absolutely nothing of any worth to anyone—making an even worse fool of herself than she had at the start of watch, if that were possible. She started to shake her head to clear her thoughts, then regretted it when it detonated a chain reaction of throbbing through her aching skull. She kept her head still with an effort, acknowledged the wristcom alert, and called up her task list. It shimmered to life above her wristcom, shining emerald lines in the gloom of the maintenance tube, reflecting off the curved gray walls.

Amelie gave up scrolling through the task list at *Item 43: Ensure all tube cabling apertures are free of dust and debris.* Clearly this was a list that was never meant to be completed, only to keep the assigned specialist busy right up until the end of watch. She double-checked her safety harness, sturdy black webbing secured tightly around her middle and under her rear, its integrated hook and tether built into the airlock just overhead, then sighed and called up *Item 1: Check all status alerts from Auxiliary Maintenance Tube Stations Alpha through November.* Station Alpha's screen was barely a meter from her face, and peering down into the darkness below her boots, she could just make out the shelf projecting from the tube's side that was, more than likely, Station Bravo, and then another below that. She heaved a sigh and tapped Station Alpha's screen; it flared to life, wrenching a pained squint out of her, and informed her that *All Alpha maintenance interlocks are in Status: Ready or Status: Inactive. Proceed?*

The maintenance tube's diameter was broader than her outstretched arms on both sides by a good two meters, and the noise of the ship wasn't much more than a subliminal hum behind its thick walls. Only the faint glow of the station screens, and the occasional running light of some piece of equipment she didn't yet know the meaning of, broke the tube's soothing darkness. The air, whispering past her face under the pressure of the ship's ventilation system, smelled cool and dry with a hint of machine oil, soothing in its familiarity. By the time she reached Station November, the throbbing in her temples had receded to a barely perceptible ache.

Station November's screen blared violent red just under her outstretched fingers; Amelie recoiled, choking off a shriek, and her boot slipped off the rung below her and kicked the wall beside it, knocking her completely off the ladder. She flailed madly—at *nothing*, there was *nothing to grab onto!*—she spun out from the wall, her safety harness tether snapping taut, then slammed back into the tube wall beside the ladder hard enough to knock the breath out of her lungs. She scrabbled for the ladder's sides, found them and clutched them with her gloved hands, heaving for air. Black spots danced in front of her eyes.

Sound erupted from Station November's crimson screen; Amelie forced her shocked brain to listen. "—EMERGENCY, all hands, ALL SHIP EMERGENCY! ALL—"

And then it stopped. The crimson screen dissolved back into the soft gray glow of its standby mode; the last echoes of the roaring machine-voice of the ship's central computer faded into the humming, hissing silence of the tube itself. Amelie gaped at the screen, still shaking from the adrenaline. Her hands, sodden with sweat inside their gloves, clutched the ladder's sides. For one crazy second she wondered if she had hallucinated the whole thing.

A flicker of movement caught her eye. Her wristcom was blinking up at her—just the standard message light, a small yellow glint—she pried her hand off the ladder and tapped the screen against her chin. *MESSAGE*, read the small display. *NO HOLO AVAILABLE.* Which was odd—"Er," said Amelie, then swallowed hard against her dry throat. "Hello?"

"Who is this?" The voice snapping out from the wristcom's tiny speaker was sharp and unfamiliar. "Who *is* this, you'd better answer!"

Amelie obediently opened her mouth, then shut it tight as a trap. And maybe she was being stupid, but regs were regs, and they'd been hammered into her head over and over—"The seething seas ceaseth," she whispered instead, hoarsely.

"What—" The voice cut off, mid-word; Amelie's stomach twisted into miserable knots.

But then a new voice spoke. "And the seething sea sufficeth us." This voice was older, masculine—vaguely familiar; she thought she ought to know it…

"Acknowledged," Amelie whispered. *Please tell me this is a security drill, and I just passed it.*

"Well done…specialist," said the almost familiar voice, after a brief hesitation. "*Is* this a specialist?"

"Yes," said Amelie faintly. "Specialist E-2 Amelie Larue. Auxiliary Engineering section, third watch."

"Where are you, Larue?"

"In the Auxiliary Engineering maintenance tube."

"What?" That was the edged feminine voice from before. "What's she doing in there? We ran a full inspection less than three weeks ago, it's not due for another check til—"

"That really doesn't matter now, Johanssen," cut in the man's voice, the voice Amelie was now sure she ought to know—certainly she knew the name he'd dropped. Though Lieutenant Commander Johanssen, Chief Engineer, had never deigned to personally address anyone in Auxiliary Engineering's third watch section before now— "Larue, I need you to stay calm, because we've got a problem," and finally the lagging synapses in her brain closed and of course she knew that voice.

"Yes, sir," Amelie got out. "Captain Herne, sir. What problem, sir?"

"You're probably not aware of this, but besides the usual passenger complement, we agreed to take on a special set of passengers—political prisoners and their families, very high-ranking political prisoners. There wasn't universal agreement about that disposition, and it's safe to say *they* certainly didn't agree with it—" It was so strange, to hear that voice that delivered the ship-wide announcements with such cool equanimity, sound so sardonic, so *human* now. "—They had no interest in leaving Earth's solar system. And now they've sabotaged the ship."

"But," broke in Amelie, forgetting all her military courtesy, "how…what…"

"Oh, they had to have had help doing it, from both outside and inside the ship. If any of us survive this mess, the investigation will be ugly." He exhaled, loudly enough that the wristcom speaker picked it up. "But what they clearly didn't have was a full picture of shipboard life. They didn't know, for example, that the captain's and chief engineer's quarters are on a different ventilation system than the rest of the ship—and so are the ship's maintenance tubes. Right now, the only people still conscious aboard ship besides those prisoners are me, Lieutenant Commander Johanssen—and you. They did manage to lock out all cabin accesses to the rest of the physical ship and the electronic systems, but weren't able to do the same to the personal communications network—which they likely thought didn't matter, as unconscious people can't use wristcoms—but that means we have *you*, Larue. In the auxiliary maintenance tube. With direct access to all of Auxiliary Engineering's stations."

Amelie eyed Station November's screen, then gave it a tentative tap with one gloved finger. The cool pearlescence of its standby mode didn't so much as flicker in response. She craned her neck back, peering back up the tube, and realized for the first time that all the running lights peppering the tube walls, those cheerful yellow sparkles, had gone out. It was far darker in the tube now; Amelie hadn't appreciated before how much illumination those running lights had given. "All the screens seem to be shut down in here too, sir—"

Johanssen's voice broke in, over the captain's: "We can get around that. I can walk you through that. Sir, what about—wait, we'll be right back, Larue." Both voices cut off, leaving Amelie alone in the blackness of the maintenance tube.

The deep humming of the ship that had so soothed her before had died down to a nearly imperceptible whisper. Amelie could hear herself breathing, and the faint beat of her own pulse in her ears. She pressed one gloved palm flat against the curving tube wall beside Station November—it was solid, unmoving, *real*. But…

Sabotage?

She had never heard of an interstellar ship being sabotaged—orbital stations, shuttles, and of course planet-based transport, yes; it didn't happen every day but it *did* happen—because nobody was stupid enough to sabotage an interstellar ship while in irrational space. Where would you *go*, if you screwed the ship up beyond repair? Interstellar ships had lifeboats, sure—but the chances of anyone actually being able to find and retrieve one in deep space, especially if the mothership was destroyed, were infinitesimal. Sabotage—the word kept bouncing off in the inside of her skull, the syllables tangling together into nonsense and unreality. *Sabotage…*

After what seemed subjectively like eternity but was probably only five minutes, Amelie's wristcom blinked yellow once more. "Larue," said Johanssen, tone now brisk and businesslike, "I want you to reach under the nearest station screen and feel for a physical latch—there should be one on the bottom left." Amelie groped around beneath the screen, then realized she'd never be able to feel anything through her glove. She stripped it off and stuffed it into her harness belt, then slid her bare fingers along the screen's smooth, icy base.

"Found it, ma'am—I think." With a sharp click, the screen swung out wide, nearly clipping Amelie in the jaw. "Yeah—*yes*, ma'am, I've got it open."

"There should be a set of wires in the topmost bracket behind the screen. Find the blue one, pull it out and plug it into your wristcom's download port."

Blue was a little hard to determine with nothing but her wristcom's faint backlighting to guide her, but Amelie didn't waste the Chief Engineer's time telling her so—only one of the wires had the right end to fit into her wristcom port anyway, and if that wasn't the right one, they were out of luck. She plugged it in, then squeaked in surprise when Station November's screen, now angled away from her, suddenly lit in a cascade of red and yellow bars. "Ma'am! The—"

"That's right." Johanssen's satisfaction was evident. "Okay—now, I'll guide you through the menus."

The screens weren't ones Amelie had ever seen before—*root directory accesses*, Johanssen called them—but as Amelie waded through them, she began to understand how they worked. Unlike the standard maintenance menus, they didn't assume that the operator was as dumb as a rock. Anyone navigating these menus *had* to know the ship's terminology, and Amelie was glad she hadn't skipped out on the required reading for her Auxiliary Engineering interstellar rating. Johanssen seemed very interested in the ship's environmental systems…

"Larue." The captain broke back in. The trace of humor that had softened his voice before was gone. "The saboteurs have done a job on the atmospheric controls. They've managed to lock them down under an Admiralty eyes-only cipher. The bad gas mix they used on the rest of the crew and passengers and the good mix they're enjoying in the brig—and Johanssen and I are enjoying in our cabins, and you in the auxiliary tube—are inalterable. Which means that even though we can probably get through our personal cabin controls to get our own doors to open, we'd never be able to get to the emergency suit lockers outside our cabins and into the suits before we passed out."

Amelie stared at Station November's screen, now showing a schematic of the brig. She'd only ever seen the brig once, on her initial onboarding tour, but—"Did they lock access to *their* doors?" Amelie heard herself ask aloud, abruptly.

"Of course not," said Johanssen's voice, sharper than irritation alone could have made it. "As a matter of fact, the *first* thing they did, according to the log, was unlock it—they probably took care of the brig watch personally," said Johanssen with a faint choking sound of rage.

"So why can't we just vent their atmosphere? All the physical controls—the door locks, the *airlock*—" Because she had remembered that the brig had its own airlock, for isolated prisoner transfer, the brig commander had told them on their tour. "The rapid decompression will knock them all out—"

"What good would *that* do *us*? And airlocks don't work like that, specialist. You ought to know that by now," Johanssen snapped.

"But I'm looking at the brig maintenance screen right now, ma'am—there's an override procedure here for venting the entire brig, for decontamination."

A pause. Then, "She's right, she's *right*, and once the ship realizes part of itself has depressurized, it'll repressurize the whole rest of the ship with the standard mix!" Johanssen broke off. "But that protocol doesn't override the physical access settings on the doors, and the decontamination procedure doesn't allow a reset without the captain's personal authorization. We won't be able to re-air the brig until you can physically get to it, captain."

Another silence. Then, "We have to do it," said the captain. "You know what their choice of sabotage now means, right before inversion point. Someone's on their way out here to pick them up. And the best way they can hope to get away with this is to destroy the ship utterly after they disembark—they can claim the ship was lost in irrational space. That does happen…"

"Their families are in the brig with them," said Johanssen, sounding like an entirely different woman from the one that had been barking orders at Amelie just a few minutes before.

"Yes," said the captain. "I know."

Their families are in there with them.

Their families—Amelie thought of her own mouth opening, speaking, and wished somebody had stapled it shut the day she'd been born. Johanssen had taken her own bad idea, the babbling of an idiot, a *hungover* idiot, and turned it into a good idea—a *good* idea that was suddenly going to be the trigger of any number of actual deaths, dead people—*children?* Were there children in there? Babies?

"Larue." It was the captain again. Amelie jerked upright; her safety harness creaked in protest at the sudden movement. "How old are you?"

"Twenty. Sir," she whispered.

Silence, then, "We'll do this together. This is by my order, Larue. My responsibility, not yours. On my mark. At my command." Amelie stared at Station November's root directory display, at the small orange rectangle marked *Brig Decontamination Protocol: WARNING: THIS ACTION CANNOT BE COUNTERMANDED.*

"Three—"

Their families are in there with them.

"Two—"

We have to do it.

"One—"

They'll destroy the ship utterly after they disembark.

"Now."

Amelie pressed the rectangle with her bare fingertip. The orange pulsed once, then darkened; the WARNING message dissolved, then new letters appeared: *DECONTAMINATION IN PROGRESS.*

The captain spoke again, but Amelie wasn't listening—oh, she *would* listen, soon enough; it was her duty. *I, Amelie Larue, do solemnly swear that I will support and defend against all enemies, foreign and domestic; that I will obey the orders of the officers appointed over me*—was she choking to death, all of a sudden? That would be fitting—no, she was crying; she rubbed her ungloved hand viciously hard against her cheeks, smearing the hot wetness into her skin. *Are they dead yet? How long does it take to die, from decompression?* She couldn't remember.

The Captain was speaking. Amelie dragged her wrist up to her ear. "—basic monitoring on Johanssen's wristcom, the atmospheric composition outside the cabins is starting to stabilize in normal range. Don't try to leave the maintenance tube til we send someone to get you—Larue? Are you listening to me?"

"Yes, sir," Amelie said dully. "I'm listening." She realized she was gripping her safety harness tightly enough to hurt with her bare hand—gripping the latch release; she looked down, at the endless darkness beneath her booted feet. The auxiliary maintenance tube ran the entire length of the ship. Her fingers twitched on the latch release, then stilled. *That* wouldn't bring back those families. And she probably didn't deserve such an easy out.

"—a hero, Specialist Larue. You—"

Amelie shut off her wristcom, fixed her tear-blinded eyes on the now-unseeable airlock entrance far above, and began the long, slow climb back up to the top.

Bone and Acid and Rushing Waves

ADDISON SMITH

Addison Smith has blood made of cold brew and flesh made of chocolate. He spends most of his time writing about fish, birds, and cybernetics, often in combination. His fiction has appeared in *Fantasy Magazine*, *Fireside Magazine*, and *Daily Science Fiction*, among others. Find him on Twitter @AddisonCSmith. "Bone and Acid and Rushing Waves" meditates on the psychology of combat. This story originally appeared in *Troopers*, edited by the inimitable Eric Fomley.

NOVA CARRIED HER CAPTAIN'S head at her waist as a reminder of what waited beyond the blast-shield doors. The creatures cleaned it to perfection, leaving a skull acid-eaten and bone white, just as she had found it in the corridor. His body had long gone down the ventilation shaft, spread to the nooks and crannies of the ship and devoured by the enemy. All he left was his head, his off-duty flannel waving on torn metal.

SHE FELT THE SKULL at her side. It was easy work to slip a chain through his eye socket and loop a carabiner to her hip. She didn't know why she did it. It was disgusting, vile. It didn't feel right to leave him.

"Malloy," her comm crackled, "I see your position. Rendezvous through that door."

The voice belonged to the skull at her hip, and the captain who had once lived in it. Still, it chat-tered through her earpiece, a perfect rendition of his voice. She didn't question it anymore. She had seen too much; she had done too much. It was a trick, but she couldn't be sure what part. They were in her head. But which part was the trick? The voice? The skull at her hip? Hell, the entire corridor, her entire life? Was it all a dream concocted by psychedelic excretions and insect mindplay? She imagined fluids dripping from pincers just beyond the door. The more she imagined them, the more she heard them.

"Roger," Nova said beneath her breath. Her suit hummed as it tried to feed her air and failed. Her breath fogged inside her helmet. The suits were strong, but the bugs were new, their acid untested. It ate through at her waist and splashed over her view from a point-blank kill shot. She still saw the creature slump, fall, crash in a chitinous mess to the floor as she shook and cried. The glass bubbled where its acids sprayed. She could only just smell it, a sign it had made it all the way through. She popped the clasp at the back of her neck and threw the helmet useless to the ground.

The chattering of the corridor intensified and raised her skin into itching gooseflesh. She hefted her rifle and toyed with the magazine.

Her comm crackled in her ear and she smiled. "Captain," she said, voice trailing into a whisper. She didn't know if she was talking to the skull or the comm that led her to that door, through a labyrinth of confused bodies. Only one of them answered.

"Nova," her captain said. "Where are you? Requesting aid." The sounds of battle filtered through the comm in static bursts. Gunfire cracked beyond the door. Nothing was real. Her captain was dead. Her team was dead. She only smiled.

"Did I ever tell you about my brother?" she asked, ignoring the constant sounds of report. "My baby brother, Seth. He was just a kid."

She smiled down at her feed, her rifle, the scorched metal of the floor. Even with tears in her eyes, she smiled.

"He fell," she said. "Earthside. Off one of the big dams that powered the old city. We weren't supposed to be there. I was supposed to be watching him."

The comm crackled like rushing waves. She didn't need to say it. If it was an illusion, the bugs would only use it. If it was real she was wasting time. Still, the memory washed through her now and she needed to put words to it to explain her actions.

"I leave people, Captain. I abandon friends. I've spent my life letting people down."

Shots fired beyond the door and she stared at it as acid dripped through in tiny rivers. If she ran now she could get away. She could die somewhere else on the ship, stage her final stand anywhere else.

Someone screamed and she clenched her teeth. It wasn't real. They weren't real.

Her tears were. Her guilt was.

Nova rested her right hand on the skull at her side, fingertips burning in the light acid residue.

"No more," she said. "I'm not leaving."

She swiveled her rifle on its shoulder strap and picked up her helmet for whatever protection it was. When she slid it over her head the smell abated, replaced by rushing air as her suit attempted to pressurize. She unhooked the carabiner and set her captain's head on the floor, empty eyes watching the door.

She raised her rifle and hovered her fingers over the door's activation panel.

"See you soon," her comm crackled.

She smiled. "See you soon, Captain."

She opened the door.

Something Else

CONRAD GARDNER

"Something Else" is original to *Bullet Points*, and it shows how being different—being set aside for violence—has such a profound effect on individuals. Conrad Gardner's fiction has previously been published by *Martian: The Magazine of Science Fiction Drabbles*, *Superlative Literary Journal*, and *White Cat Publications*. He has stories appearing in forthcoming editions of *Sci Phi Journal* and *Impossible Worlds*. Writing is an attempt for him to channel his neurodiverse mania into something useful—the results remain to be seen—and to survive. He can be reached @conblogs1 on Twitter.

Warning: contains adult themes and nudity.

THERE WAS AN EXPLOSION. A Big Bang. It gave birth to a life and a death. So many deaths.

IT KILLED ME. NOT then, not billions of years ago. But I died from an explosion. I'm dead. I was killed on a battlefield on Ares. It wasn't what people would call a valiant death. I stepped on a mine and was shot several times until I bled out. I screamed. A lot. In those final moments, I laughed. Not that the pain was funny. See, in the beginning, we were all brought into this world by the Big Bang, and then came out of our mother's wombs kicking and screaming.

I was brought out of this world by a Big Bang, and sent screaming, though only one of my legs was kicking, spasming out of some stimulation of my nerves. The other came off in the blast.

But that was then. This is now.

My eyes open. Seeing isn't like I remembered. I swear there's static in my vision, like a TV. Around me I see the people in lab coats, doctors. These aren't the army medics. They're different, don't wear any signs of rank. Half of one person's face is metal. They look at me and I want to hide. I suppose it doesn't matter, because I can't get up, and they're above me. They're holding a tablet. "Hello," they say.

Something happens in my eyes and next to the doctor (I think they're a doctor), a photo of them shows up. It says "DR IRAKARI" and I try pulling my head away from the screen, but the image follows me and I realize it's inside my eyes, inside my head.

"Sorry, you must be seeing who I am. That's okay, Mezar." They know my name.

I try wriggling my toes, getting off whatever table this is, but something's stopping me, and I can't feel my skin on the table. I look, and there's a rod sticking out of where my leg used to be. A drone with a blowtorch is welding something onto it. I open my mouth to scream.

Irakari taps their tablet and my scream is muted. The sound disappears from my mouth. "Are you going to be quiet? We are trying to help you," they say. It strikes me that there's no point in fighting this: I'm already dead. I surrender, not to the forces of some armed threat, but to a doctor in a lab coat, their only weapon a fourteen square-inch tablet. "Do you remember Ares, Mezar, what happened there? The mine?" I nod, start to speak, but no sound comes out. "Oh sorry about that," they say, and give me my voice back.

"I died, didn't I?"

They nod. "Yes, and this is your after. Not your afterlife. But your after-something. We've brought you back."

"I thought I was meant to be dead," I say.

"We're all meant to die, but some of us are meant for a second chance, something more."

"And you decide that?"

"Yes," Irakari says, "I saw your file, and I thought it was a waste of a life for you to be killed in a battle on Ares. We won, by the way." I blink. "Your brain was intact, and your foundation was strong." Irakari eyes my body.

"So what do I do now, go back to combat?"

Irakari scoffs. "No, you're much too sophisticated for that. You will be, at any rate. We thought you might be more suited for assassination, if you're still interested in serving your continent." I say I am, more because I figure Irakari can kill me with that tablet rather than my want-

ing to. I already gave these people fifteen years of my life, joined when I was sixteen. But I've been given a chance to live again. Who wouldn't take that? "Wonderful," Irakari claps their hands and helps me up, taking my arms. They steady me, and the shock of my half-metal leg is gone, replaced by something else.

My body is a mishmash of exposed metal and flesh. Wires and patches of skin make a quilt of my torso and legs. Two hollows sit where my breasts used to be. My face is untouched. It looks better than before, the skin smoother. Irakari puts their hand on my shoulder. It's cold at the touch and I register the metal on my deltoid. "Your brain was intact and your body, well, that's not as important as you might think. It can be changed as and when it needs to. It is a mere blank canvas," they wave a hand over my body. I ask what they've done to me. "We've made you the perfect operative. Why let your body, your face, your"—they look at the gaps in my chest—"equipment hold you back? Why, when you can pick and choose?" I don't understand and say nothing, but Irakari moves on and tells me that my first assignment is ready for when they finish building my body.

Before putting me under, switching me off, they say, "You'll get used to this. You're a survivor." But I'm not. I've died; there's a difference. There's a noise before I sleep. It's like an explosion.

I wake up again and stand without any problems this time. I have a pair of toned pectorals where my breasts were before. My body has something that resembles skin coating it, though I feel the movement of wires when I wiggle my toes. There's something between my legs, bulging. It sticks out above my navel, sits on the metal slab. It's not uncomfortable. Irakari comes to my side, says my waking up is something amazing. They have the same substance on my body covering the metal half of their face. "You've woken up of your own accord, very impressive. How are you finding it?"

"I don't know," I say. Irakari says it doesn't

matter because I'm being sent on my first mission. I am to kill a foreign diplomat and leave their death in a humiliating circumstance. I ask about the humiliating circumstance, and Irakari says I'll know what to do when the time comes. When I get the information on my display, I say okay, and they hand me some clothes. I'm airdropped into some desert location, a warehouse. It's dark, but I can see everything. I look up to the stars, see the bull constellation overhead. I'm on Taurus.

Infiltrating the diplomat's house is easy enough. I can see the floorplan as I infiltrate it, courtesy of the imaging, and my body moves quieter than someone who's spent fifteen years shooting people in battlefields should be able to. Irakari says it's a "stealth program." I make it to the diplomat's bedroom. Their guards never get a chance to see me enter.

The room is covered in silk. I scan the room and pick up a person in the bathroom. They are one-hundred percent flesh, unlike me. My eyes scan my body and tell me that eighty percent of it is not human tissue. The diplomat's shower is running and the steam seeps in through the bottom of the door. I sit on the bed and wait for them to come out, but the water keeps running. I step toward the door, silenced gun at the ready, but my thermal sensors are screwed, and I can't sense them when they open the bathroom door. They aren't surprised. They smile. My gun is aiming for their head and they don't care. "I knew this time would come soon," they say.

"I'm—"

"You are to kill me and leave my death in a humiliating circumstance, I know. I helped write your programming."

"I thought you were a politician."

"I am, but I also helped design you." I didn't know I needed designing. "Making something as unique as you is difficult. You are something else, unlike any previous operative. Not quite human, not quite a robot."

"What does that make me?"

"You are like I said, something else." I say I

won't kill them if they can tell me more about myself, because everything that's happened to me is a mystery. I can bypass security systems with half a thought, but this seems natural now, is natural. Then my body seizes after I speak. "You have to kill me, and I have to die. It is the way. I will not stop you. All I ask is one thing." They pause. "I want you to grant me a last wish, a gift from a creation to its creator. Lie with me, before you do what you must."

I do what they ask. At first I don't understand how it works, how I get the appendage to work, but it does, and I am copulating with someone else. This should all feel strange to me, and inside my mind it does, but my body seems no different, and I'm more used to the sensation than someone built like I used to be would think. My hand still holds the gun during the act. I can't tell whether I'm enjoying myself, or my programming is telling me that I am, but in the moment I don't care: it's glorious.

When I finish, they thank me and say I can do what I have to. I move the gun a few inches and shoot them through the bottom of the head. The pillows are stained red.

I leave their corpse in a humiliating circumstance, the words "FREEDOMIST PIG" written around the room in blood. Like before, this is clockwork to my body and I don't recognize what I've done until I finish. I leave the diplomat/programmer/person's house through the window, and have questions I want to ask when the stealth craft picks me up.

I am back in one of Irakari's labs. They turn off the news, which discusses the outrage after the diplomat's killing. It seems to have been caused by the enemy. They were on our side, and I wrote those words and know it was me, but my body is comfortable with having done it, it experiences no revulsion. Irakari sits opposite me. "You performed excellently," they say. "The seeds are sown now, and we can do what we must to win this war."

"How does this help? How did I help in any of this?"

"You've blurred the borders of the human body and technology, and are defeating the enemy in a more efficient way." I don't understand them. "Killing the diplomat is going to motivate more people to join the fight. We'll have more funding, and you can be upgraded, sent across enemy lines to reach your full potential and execute their higher-ups."

"What does that mean?"

"We'll give you the equipment that is required to attract your target, and you will eliminate the leaders, the politicians. Will you continue the mission?"

I nod, but don't know if I want to or if Irakari's making me. Is this programming or my choice? I guess it doesn't matter. "By the way, did you enjoy granting their last wish?" Irakari chuckles, and tells me that they enjoyed the show. They watched me do it, and I remember my display, how my body seized when I offered not to kill the diplomat. It made sense they'd be watching their new experiment, but controlling it? Did they program those movements or did I perform them myself?

Over the next few months, my cup size changes from B, to H, to D. My penis size changes from the global average on Pisces to above-average on Ares. Walking around with that much is uncomfortable, but it gets the attention of the target. Whatever the targets like, I can be. I am the object of their desire and their demise.

When I've finished, when they've surrendered themselves to me, I kill them. I use a gun that's inserted into my hand and can be unveiled at my wrist, the first modification Irakari made after the green light to go across lines was given. The short explosion as the bullet fires makes my artificial heart run faster. The explosion, once again, comes at the end. The targets are lucky. They're not brought out of this world kicking and screaming. They get to die in bliss.

I've been given more body parts than you can think of, but they always change. None of them feel right for me. Not the fact that my body's been changed. On the contrary, I'm enjoying the new appendages I've worn, and changing is enjoyable for me. It gives me the freedom to try everything, see what I'm comfortable in.

What makes them not feel right is that I don't think I have any choice in the matter, not really. I try to think about my old body, but I can't remember what that is anymore. I check my systems each day. I'm still twenty-percent human tissue. Some of Irakari's assistants tell me how great I am, that I'll be the person to end this war, and whenever I hear this, I remember what the diplomat said.

I'm not human. I'm not a robot. I'm something else. I don't know what I am, but I'm something, and I think about death when I'm not causing it. The fact that I have died is no longer a shock to me. Seeing death gives me a numb feeling. Most of my sensations are like this. I only wish that my body, how it is now, could feel like my own.

I am unique to everything else in this world, and I am alone.

And Kill Them

WILLIAM R. D. WOOD

William R. D. Wood weaves a punchy but compelling tale about perceptions and warfare in this story. Wood traces his love of science fiction and horror back to a childhood filled with *Space: 1999* reruns, frequent visits to the *Night Gallery*, and a worn-out copy of *Dune*. Much of his work is influenced by eight years of service in the U.S. Navy, five years in steel mills, and a thousand years of observations along the way. A good writing day finds him at any of several overlooks on the Blue Ridge Parkway, deeply immersed in new works of cosmic horror. Will lives with his wife, children, and assorted ghosts in an old farmhouse turned backward to the road. "And Kill Them" originally appeared in *Battlespace*.

KHALID FLEXED HIS NEW hand inside the gauntlet of his assault weapon. The grip's texture was rough and the cold of the nitrogen chiller next to his thumb felt exactly as it had before the last combat drop. The docs did good work. Sometimes that bothered him.

"GOT THAT LOOK IN your eye again."

"What look?" asked Khalid, flipping down his visor. The other noncom locked into position beside him as the tram gained speed. The slipfield in the launch tube was already frosting the air and the tang of ozone stung his nose and throat.

"Like you're dwelling on retirement again." Cooper shook his head. "Heaven ain't for us, Staff Sergeant."

"You can secure that shit," snapped Khalid. But Cooper was right. He really could go for a simpler life. The annual rejuvenations when he re-upped were nice, but what good was living a few hundred years when you had to spend it with a bunch of assholes? He sneered.

"Yep, thought so," said Cooper.

Khalid could *hear* the grin spreading across the smug bastard's face.

Navy types watched from observation platforms as the tram sped along. *That* was living. Drive the big ships within range, then shoot the ground-pounders through slipspace at the target world. Same tech that pushed billion-ton warships through subspace could also deliver troops across short distances without the need for landers. Space jockeys never even broke a sweat.

A group of women in civvies smiled and waved as they flew past.

Khalid glanced at Cooper as the other noncom waved back. A green icon pinged above Cooper's head—Kahlid's IFF system identifying Cooper as a friendly. Someday he was going to have the techies program in another color to designate *moron*. He smirked.

"Okay, boys and girls," said Cooper to their squads. "Links on. Weapons hot."

Khalid's own link tingled to life, data scrolling across his vision, delivered to his brain by nanofilaments and synzymes through the base of his skull. Basic drop site info, weapons settings, and local bio profiles.

"You gotta be kidding," said Cooper. "Where does *that* even evolve?"

The tunnel convulsed into a mass of crisscrossing discharges. Needles ripped through Khalid.

And his feet hit the ground.

He sprinted ahead to clear the drop for the troops flashing into existence behind him. The panorama assaulted his senses. Golden rings arced up from the horizon, bisecting a violet sky filled with iridescent clouds. Smells, pungent and sweet, bypassed his respiratory supplements. An ocean of orange and yellow grasses shimmered, ringing like wind chimes in the breeze.

Khalid had never imagined a place so…heavenly.

"Go to exotic places," murmured Cooper through their noncom link.

Blurs of blue and green sprang skyward from the grasses. Feathery tentacles writhed beneath veined butterfly wings. The closest bore down on them, a twisted rod in its tentacles growing brighter as it closed. *Meet exotic people.*

His field of vision filled with icons, pinging into an oncoming storm of red.

Khalid smiled, his new hand unleashing hell.

Closing Time

T. M. THOMAS

T. M. Thomas is a lawyer and writer son of an enlisted U.S. Air Force dad and three enlisted U.S. Army combat uncles, living the middle-aged life in the middle of nowhere in upstate New York. "Closing Time" is original to *Bullet Points*, and is as surprising as it is brief. Sometimes war does that, throws complete curveballs.

"THE BAY NEEDS TO be closed, Captain," I said for the third time.

RY SOBCHAK SMILED THAT infamous charmer's white smile down from the top of the bird. The big triangle of a ship was too large to crawl up after him, unless I wanted to chase him around the turrets for a half hour. He had a rag in one hand and a bottle of metal cleaner in the other as he sat astride the gun mount just forward of the cockpit. Two empty liquor bottles were on the ground beside the cruiser, one smashed and the other just empty.

"You married, Airman?"

"No, sir. Now please come down. The techs need to do postflight checks on these ships."

He leaned back. He was lanky and lean, perfectly shaped for fitting in the cockpits of the A-23. Rumor was they'd even built the newest ones around him, as the prototype build. His leathery face and curly hair, lighter in streaks and at the tips, looked like a man who spent his days ranching, like my dad, and not aboard a carrier past Io.

"Son, one thing to learn. Rules don't apply. You do what she wants, she'll be mad you didn't do more. You do what you want, she'll be twice as mad."

"Sir, I'll remember that. Now if you'll come down? It's 0145 and we need to secure this bay."

He stood, weaving a little as he swung his long legs over the gunmount. He slipped a little and the metal cleaner clanked against the long barrel.

"Son, I've done fifty-eight missions on this tour alone. I've rained death and destruction down on the enemies of the Confederation. I got scrubbed from today's flight because she told them I was a drunk. I'm not crawling home to her on your say so!"

He slammed his hand down on the barrel, again. There was a little click as the metal can fell away, then clanks as it bounced off the armored hull and onto the corrugated metal floor. "Damn it," he muttered, slamming his empty hands down on the metal so it rang through the empty bay.

"You don't need to go home," I started to say, when there were five more clicks.

"What?" he started, but I was already running. It was only a few yards to the emergency blast doors, already grinding shut, but it felt like an hour of running in cold Terran mud before I put the three feet of metal between me and the bay.

The nanotech shell in the barrel didn't do any-thing as dramatic as explode. Captain Sobchak didn't have time to do anything before the little cone of clicking metal extended a few feet from the barrel. The techs would have found the misfired shell and cleaned it out properly, if he'd listened.

The skeleton fell on the floor, breaking into hundreds of pieces and mixing into the broken pieces of the liquor bottles. The metal swarm fell to dust, coating the few feet it had covered with a silver snow that reflected all the pale emergency lights back at me.

I sucked in air, terrified I'd feel my lungs start-ing to dissolve with any nanotech bugs I'd in-haled, then reached for my radio.

The Golden Rays of the Morning Sun

Marc A. Criley

"The Golden Rays of the Morning Sun," which originally appeared in *Abyss & Apex*, is a beautiful and poignant exploration of the tragedy of warfare for the human soul, but also the triumph of the human spirit. Marc A. Criley avidly read fantasy and science fiction for over forty years before deciding to try his hand at writing it. He has since been published in *Beneath Ceaseless Skies*, *Galaxy's Edge*, and elsewhere. It is never too late to start writing. Marc and his wife "manage" a household of cats in the hills of North Alabama. Marc spouts off about writing, space, Alabama, and other shiny things as @MarcC@wandering.shop.

A BLUE-VIOLET FLASH. And sparks, streams of sparks; immersing me in all-the-colors-of-the-rainbow sparks. A dull rumble punches through the helmet's attenuators. I'm weightless, floating … and stupidly lucid. Weightless, not space weightless, but arcing through the air until the hard stop at the end weightless. Cartwheeling. Angry. Furious.

I CAREEN ACROSS THE tarmac …

STRAPS ABRADING BARE SKIN. Belted to a cot. The evac dustoff. Streaking barrages of red and gold, roiling black explosions, blue-white flashes, sledgehammers slamming the hull, corkscrew spins. Shrieking engines. Rolling once, twice, again, now again, now again, losing count. Coming to. Fading out. In. Out. In. Out. Flashes and screams—me, others. Out.

EYES OPEN. POINT LIGHTS, star-like scattered and flickering amongst scaffolding, struts, conduits, cables. Weightless, space weightless now. Up is down and right is left as I tumble up and over and around; winding a serpentine path through unwalled corridors. I'm strapped to an autonomous gurney, hooked into IV pumps and restraints, coasting through hospital ship med-spaces. I pass doctors, nurses, cyb techs—bloody gowns cinched at wrist and waist. Robo-docs. Burnt meat smell. Vomit. Shit. Doctors snapped into foot restraints; doctors and techs hand-over-handing, riding tow cables. Whispering, watching, scared. Amber glows, flashing LEDs, flat tones, med machine beeps silenced. No need here for red strobes and howling klaxons.

A gurney harness hauling an armored torso shoots past; arm cuffs tourniquet one truncated arm and the flapping shreds of the other. A lone leg windmills in the breeze. The helmeted head lolls around, then stops and rocks violently. Screaming? Maybe. Hard to tell. It cuts ahead of me. Hey! Trailing a red haze. I pass out.

Open my eyes to a hovering cyb tech. I see cyb eyes, gold ones, no pupils or irises—featureless gold discs.

A golden memory of that last, good day.

"You're gonna be fine," the tech says, breaking the memory as he adjusts the restraints. "SA's got an eye, legs, everything you need to make a body new, better'n new. We'll have ya back poundin' dirt in no time. We're even gonna reskin you. Latest tech, super stealthy, you'll be good for *years*. Now you go on back to sleep."

A DOZEN YEARS AGO that cyb," Dr. Emmedi vaguely waves at me, "was state-of-the-art, but now…it's all legacy. You're obsolete, Mika, to put it bluntly. Special Acquisitions is transitioning to a new baseline. Your experience is irreplaceable and we want you on board, so you're up for cerebral extraction and rehost." The doctor smiles, creaks back in the worn mesh corporate

standard military contractor office chair. A vent fan purrs overhead. "And to be perfectly frank, your cyb's being end-of-lifed so this is your only path forward. It'll be a win for Special Acquisitions, for our customers and obviously—with your medical and combat history—for you. Win win win."

The staff doctor drones on about specs and performance tuning. I tune out and flick through cyb readings of ambient light flux, EM background noise, room temperature gradient. I infrared scan Emmedi—heated brow, a little sweaty, a little anxious—then push the cyb data aside. The office is small, windowless. Framed diplomas and images—2D, 3D, animated—jostle for wall space. The good doctor posing with SA-uniformed men and women, the occasional suit or lab coat breaking the monotony. No family pictures, no informalities. I focus back on the doctor, scan a fast replay to catch up.

"Why don't I have a say in this?" I interrupt. "I've got enough cyb—arm, eye, half my guts—everything from the waist down. This isn't even my own skin." I ripple orange and black stripes down each bare dermakinetic forearm. "Isn't this enough? I'm barely hanging onto human as it is. This is enough. I'm fine as is, I don't need, or want, to *rehost*."

Emmedi waves away my refusal. "We're sorry, but hybrid cyb maintenance is no longer cost effective. As I said, it's being end-of-lifed. Your biology is degrading, and while cyb augments those functions, in the long run it's a losing battle. You're at a tipping point, it's why you're up for rehost. And I'll be honest, Mika, I'm surprised at your reaction. That transplant you got as a child saved your life, *gave* you a life, but it and the rest of your biology is wearing out, it's hitting the limits. Rehosting does away with limits…permanently. If I were in your shoes I'd jump at this!"

Emmedi leans forward, fixes on my gaze. "Organics are vulnerable, they degrade. Rehosting eliminates the vulnerabilities while simultaneously maximizing personal performance. Which benefits you and, not coincidentally, SA. Keep in mind the company pays for all this. Our doubling down on the investment, making this transition, results in an *exponential* leap forward, upward. We optimize the efficiency of human experience and performance."

I hold the doctor's stare, then shake it loose. "What 'human experience'? How does putting me in a machine possibly 'optimize' *human experience*?"

"It's not a 'machine,' Mika, it's a cyboront. But it's just a shell—think of it as power armor you put on and never take off—nothing changes your humanity, Mika, *nothing*. You're simply more efficient. That's a win for us, for holding the peace, for expanding market share. And for you the enhanced perception, analytics, and augmentation presages a deeper, fuller, *more human*, direct, hands-on, one-on-one experience with the world, with the universe. Makes you better at what you do. Makes you better at what *we* do. But honestly *you* are the primary beneficiary in all this, putting you on the forefront of human evolution. Sky's the limit! No, the *universe* is the limit."

I shake my head, close my eyes. *I see back to a sweaty two-day trek, diving into a cold pond, aching legs—the good kind of ache. Sleeping untented under the stars, me and Cori pointing at and whisper-naming constellations while our parents snored in the tent. Waking up early, breathlessly awaiting the first light of the morning sun.*

"No spacesuits," Emmedi enthuses, "no diving gear. Airless, poisonous, doesn't matter. Steel on bone reality. As is you've already integrated cyb electromagnetics; rehosting *multidimensionalizes* those senses, then adds more. You'll *transcend* yourself. Nothing that's *you* changes, you're rehosted to"—air quotes—"*an enhanced plane of existence* is how the cyb techs put it." The doctor chuckles. "Without the distraction of eating, sleeping, getting sick, tired, or other ailments, you're *you*—always on, fully into every moment of your life. And that," Emmedi bangs an index finger on the desk display for emphasis, "is the future. *That* is the *Future of Humanity*."

I run a diagnostic, an anatomical status flashes up. All green, one hundred percent. Just over six hundred hours of power remaining in the current power cap, based on current and predicted usage heuristics.

"And if I refuse?"

The happy grin of the pitch evaporates. There's silence, then a sigh. Finally, "That's your right. Special Acquisitions doesn't own you but it does own your cyb. If you decline to rehost your contract terminates. Your legs, arm, and optics are reclaimed—the tech is SA proprietary. The internal augmentation is safed, and you're mustered out with a full power cap. You'll have time to ... *make arrangements* before the cap zeroes. Then you're at the mercy of whatever's left of your biology, including that heart. You've been damaged, severely. You know that. To be blunt, Mika, you're half-dead right now. Cyb is the only thing keeping you alive, augmenting, filling in the gaps, but it can't heal you. Biology degrades; cyb doesn't. There's nothing you can do to stop it. Unaugmented you'd likely be dead within an hour. If you want to live, you rehost."

"So I have no choice."

Emmedi's head rolls back, another sigh slips out. "You *have* a choice, Mika, *live* or *die*. And just so you know, quite a few do hesitate at first, until they go through VRientation. Everyone comes around then, and you will too."

"But if I don't, then I die."

Emmedi shrugs. "Yes, okay, if you don't then you die." Emmedi slides and sorts folders on the desk panel, taps one. "You have forty-eight hours to check in at SA's augmentation clinic. If you don't show up for rehost, or reclamation, someone will come get you. So be a good soldier and don't break anything. And don't run, retrieval expenses come out of your pay."

O UTSIDE EMMEDI'S OFFICE IT'S night, a cold breeze steals blood warmth. Or it would if I still had human skin. Clear skies tonight. A smear of galactic core. Stars, patterns of stars. I don't know their names, don't know their patterns. Probably fought around some of them. I can call up star chart overlays, but it's been many years since I could just look up and reel off names. Years and light-years since I last saw home and the golden rays of the morning sun. Dermakinetic skin or no I shiver, rub my chest. The scars are long gone, replaced with chromatophore-infused 'smart skin.' But the heart remains. I call up a monitor, count along with each beat: one, two, three. No one, no one is going to take that away. Four, five, six…

I GRAB THE GO bag from my quarters and punch in the address of a late night bar down by the spaceport. I never arrive…at the bar. Half a klick away I preemptively break my contract: disable comms, enable transponder spoofing, illegally activate tactical stealth in a non-contract zone.

Time to go home.

I'M THREE HUNDRED KILOMETERS north of my home world's northernmost spaceport, and twenty klicks into the Preserve when a shutdown signal encoded with my serial number goes out on planetary security wideband. I ignore it—busted termination processor. Disabling the processor damaged my organ augmentation logic, so I'm dying for real now—with a hundred rough-country kilometers yet to cross. I pick at the field patch on my cyb thigh.

A half hour later the double boom of an SA atmospheric penetrator reentry rolls over the hills. The Preserve's rangers aren't going to like that. I scramble my way under heavy evergreen foliage. It will thin as I move north, but I take advantage of the thickness in these parts. Up the first ridge it's all bushwhacking, no real trails. On bare flat terrain my legs haul ass at seventy klicks, here

I'm barely managing six. An hour is spent traversing karst, ravines, boulders, sinkholes, trees, and deadfall before I clear the first ridge.

Two more double booms roll down from the sky. I bump up the tactical stealth, power reserves be damned—I've given up on a round trip. I had nearly three hundred hours of power when I stepped off the transport. But slipping out of the spaceport riding high stealth, running constant spoof, and overclocking the damaged organ augmentation dropped that to under a hundred. I hope it's enough. Yet more booms. I exhale, my breath an infrared glow.

A MEDICAL SOS BLARES out—I forgot to disable the emergency beacon. I immediately abort it, but not before a medical summary burst—including location—goes up. Diagnostics say I've lost one kidney; ten percent on the other. My heart's racing. I infuse a couple micrograms of *Flashdrive*, then run for two straight hours under full dermakinetic stealth and tactical cyb. Organ augmentation redlines as it works to clear the poison contaminating my blood. Careening up and over rocks and ridges, dodging trees living and dead; I'm a disembodied torso strapped to a roller coaster runaway gurney. I'm flying through forest and stone, and it's gonna hurt like hell when I hit the hard stop.

A NOTHER VALLEY. OR A dale. Or a hollow. Water here, a pool. Some thin ice. I crack it and wade in up to my chest. Cold, frigid. The burn in my gut subsides. Water circulates through my cyb legs, absorbs excess heat. The warmed water rises, tickles my sides and chest.

Stars burn down. I know the bright ones—Kordan, Mesran, Eliamon; and the names of ancient constellations—Blacksmith, Estevay, Coriinme, the Sails of Morning.

One more climb. Must beat the morning sun. Power reserve ticks below three hours.

I CLEAR THE LAST ridge, peer down into the Aurbem Valley; a dry rocky streamed meandering along the bottom. I see no one on the broad swale of heath, moor, or whatever the word is for ground cover and low brush. *The last good day* happened on the far side of this valley, not far from where I lean. I can almost pick out the spot. I sidle about halfway down this side of the valley, skirt the rock shelves and outcroppings, then drop and wedge myself against a boulder. I power down my legs—no more running. It's cold. Clear view in both directions. The valley bends east, opening to the circumpolar plains. Not long now. I'm sick in the gut. I turn off most diagnostics and monitors, just leave the power level display. There's enough to last past sunup. And a bit more.

A pair of legs steps into my dim vision. Boots, skin-tight pants. Can't see more. Someone lays a hand on my shoulder.

"Mika? You're Mika, right? I've been looking for you."

S O YOU'RE ONE OF them," I say.
"One of what?"

"The cost-effective, rehosted *Future of Humanity.*"

The figure cocks its head. "I wouldn't know about that. I'm Specialist Kibo Harran, on orders to retrieve you." Something is pulled out of a pocket. I can't tell if the pocket's real or just part of the machine. "Here. This is a full power cap. Plug it in."

I bat the hand away. "No."

"Don't be stupid. Your cap's almost zeroed and you're almost dead. Plug it in. You need to stay alive until a transporter arrives."

"Emmedi said it was my choice."

"A choice no one ever makes."

"Except me."

Kibo crosses his arms.

"Show me your face," I say.

"What?"

"*Let me see your face.*"

Kibo shrugs and squats in front of me. He smiles. "Happy?"

"No," I say. "Your *face.* Show me your *face.* Turn off the *dermakinetics.*"

He gazes at me for a few seconds, then the smile evaporates. As does the face, first paling to dullness. Then the features dissolve, in a moment I'm facing a gray oval in the blue-gray dawn. I barely make out shallow depressions for eyes, a nose bump, a shallow groove splitting a pair of small lip-shaped swellings. The ears are just knobs. Fibrous threads withdraw to a finger's length, then lay flat on the scalp.

"Satisfied?" the cyboront says. There's no obvious movement in the facade accompanying the voice. "Look, you're gonna be dead in a few minutes if you don't power up. This was stupid, you could've come here after the rehost, hell I'd've come with you, this place looks amazing. But we need to get you back. Take the cap." Kibo holds it out.

"No!" I shout, swinging at him, knocking his hand away. He loses his grip on the cap, it bounces a few meters down the slope. My heart bangs. Dizziness, nausea surges. I've got less than ten minutes of power left.

Kibo—robot, android, *cyboront,* whatever—stands up, steps back. "You'll die out here."

"What do you care? *Humans* die."

"We don't need to any more."

"What 'we,' Kibo? *Humans* die." I cough, taste blood. "You're not Kibo Harran. Whoever that was is just a bunch of medical waste now. That's not going to happen to me."

Kibo's cyboront body stiffens. "No. Nothing happened to *me.* You're wrong." Each word snapped off. "I am who I was. And am. In all the ways that *matter.*"

I'm unfazed. "Says who? What ways? What's left of you? A brain? Some brain stem, maybe? All micro-threaded with nanowires and augmentation networks? A little AI maybe? What part of any of that is human? Where's the *meat,* Kibo?

It's not all neurons and nanotech. It's muscle, skin, heart…" My voice catches. I swallow—tastes of blood and saliva—continue. "We're not just electrical impulses speeding over integrated silver, tantalum, and neuron meshes. You're a cyb puppet of someone who once had a life. A ghost in—"

"Shut up!"

I smile weakly. "If there's one thing you're not, Mister Future of Humanity, it's human."

"You're wrong, Mika," Kibo says, taking a step toward me, squatting back down. He pauses a moment, looks down the valley. "No, you know what? You're right, because that's all you are too." He turns back to me. "That's all we *humans* are, puppet bodies, electrical impulses spinning around the brain, the meat, exchanges of ions and electrons. I don't need a bio heart, liver, kidneys, stomach, to be human. All I need is what's in here." He taps his chest again. "That's what makes me human. I'm alert twenty-four seven, constantly aware of everything around me, taking it all in, enhanced."

He pauses, tilts his head up, listens. "I hear them," he says, "they'll be here in a couple minutes."

My heart skips a beat, I glance at the sunrise end of the valley.

"Why would I not do this?" Kibo continues, turning the blank face back to me. "Why would anyone not do this? Cyb senses and neural enhancement enrich every experience, make it deeper, more compelling, more deeply felt, more…intimate. We're sensory creatures, Mika, you and I; and a cyboront is all about *sensory immersion*."

I keep my eyes fixed on the far end of the valley. "I'm cold. Right now I'm cold. Do you get cold?"

"No, and neither will you." Kibo's blank visage takes on a dull red hue as a sliver of sun crests the horizon.

"Do you ever get hot? Tired? Sore, dull, achy?" I turn back to face him. "Do you ever get a headache? Do you slip under the water and hold your breath till everything goes red, until you see sparkling black stars?" I take a deep breath. "Do you know what it feels like to smash through a window? To be impaled on a spear of glass, feeling your heart squish and leak as it struggles to beat?" My vision becomes a watery blur. "To see the gray and black rolling in? To feel your chest tearing apart as you reach for your twin, watch the light go out of their eyes? What do you feel, 'Future of Humanity'? Do you, *can you*, feel *anything*?"

Kibo gets to his feet and steps back, then the oval of his face transforms. Open wounds appear, a smashed bloody nose, gashed temple, closed eyes swollen black. The dermakinetic skin-tight uniform morphs into naked human flesh.

One arm appears cleanly sliced off below the shoulder, the other a mangle of muscle and bone. An empty space at the hip marks where one leg used to attach, the other dangles on shredded strips of tendon and muscle. Bone shards protrude from red and blackened flesh.

I gape at him, at what's left of him, a hovering apparition of weightlessness, nakedness, and agony.

Cutting the line in a dimly lit hospital ship.

"I felt it all," the torn mouth says, the words mushed like slush on cold concrete. "No painkillers. I was forward spotter, Special Acquisitions needed me lucid, so the armor pumped me full of stims. My brain sizzling on agony and *Flashdrive*. It should've seized up. I never passed out. Hyper-awake through all of it. The evac, evasives, high gee, it's all still"—Kibo points at his chest with the arm stump—"here. Like it happened yesterday. The hospital boat, the reek of burnt iron, charred flesh. Mine, everyone's. They couldn't knock me out, no locals, no nothing. Overstimmed, couldn't put me down. Got amputated, cauterized, all live and in ultra hi-res actual reality. White steel carving up brain and body. I screamed at them to *make it stop*."

Kibo *heals* himself. The face, torso, arms and legs of a trim young Special Acquisitions contractor reappear in seconds.

"And that's what they did. I was the third prototype. Win."

I WILL NEVER GO through that again," he says. "This? The cyboront? You can crush a leg, slice off an arm, hyperslug me at point blank range, I don't care. I can do a naked atmospheric reentry from an orbiter airlock. This'll all burn off," he sweeps a hand down his body, "but if the core canister survives—and it's designed to—I survive. Just drop it in another cyboront and I'm good to go. It's all I need. It's what I want."

"But that's not what I want," I say. "It's not what I...am." I lean my head all the way back onto the cold rock, stare at the sky. "The last time I was here, it was the four of us—my parents, me, and Cori. We watched the rays sail in, then headed home. Just outside the Preserve a cargo hauler snapped an axle. Hit us head on, almost. Killed my parents. I went through the glass, took a shard in the chest. Cori was...was on life support until we got to the hospital." I lightly tap my chest. "This is Cori's heart. Cori's heart has kept me alive for the last twenty years. Cori's heart will not be carved out and tossed in some dumpster. Cori's heart, and this place, are all that I have left of home."

Kibo covers his mouth with his hand—a very human gesture.

"You had it all replaced," I say. "Fine. It's all better than new, right? For you. You went through what you went through, for sure, and I am so sorry for that; but remembering in the brain is not remembering in the bone, in the muscle, in the bile. Cori is part of me for as long as I am me. You may *remember* for a long time. But, in time, decades or centuries from now, you *will* forget."

The sun clears the ridge, crepuscular shafts of golden light arc across the sky.

I try to sit up a little straighter, find a balance point on the slope. Red sunrise shifts to orange. Two minutes left. I lock, power down my arm. That reclaims three minutes. Back up to five now.

"Mika—"

"Kibo, how human are you? You don't eat, you *recharge*. You don't shit, you *discharge*. Underwater you don't breathe, in space you don't breathe. Who keeps you alive, Kibo? How do you ever say 'no' to them? Go here, go there, fight here, fight there. 'Now here's your power cap. *Good soldier.*' You don't know who you're shooting at today, and you won't know who you're shooting at tomorrow. How long does this all go on? How long will they keep you powered up? I'll tell you—until you're *legacy*." I close my eyes, lean my head back. "Damn it Kibo, I am Cori's heart. *I* will decide to live or die as *I* see fit."

The few morning insects and birds that had been cricking and burbling stilled. Silence presses in on my ears. Kibo whispers, close, "Mika, if you die, Cori dies. Both of you." I open my eyes. Kibo is leaning down, a hand on my dead leg. "There will be *no one* left to remember," he says. A red zero power level flashes in my cyb eye, then blinks out. I lose the left half of my vision. At the end of the valley something flickers. Kibo stands up and steps out of my halved sight.

A thirty meter floating diamond of translucent amber silk curves into the valley—a golden ray shimmering in the morning sun. Its trident tail lazes behind; glittering stars wink along unseen sinews. It glides twenty meters above the dry streambed, just below eye level. Another ray appears, a few meters above and a half-dozen behind the lead, billowing along in its wake. Not flapping, not flying; but, like...water gently surging onto the sandy shore of a lake on a silent newborn day. I inhale, unaugmented, for the first time in over a decade. A shallow breath, enough. For now.

More rays enter the valley, three, four, six, ten, I lose count. A *fever* of golden rays, breathlessly silent, sparkling with each forward surge. They rise and fall like a sleeper's breath, pulse like the beat of a heart; they slip through invisible layers of air and time. A minute later the lead ray comes abreast, sails past. I start to gasp, a little. The edge of my vision grays. Cold seeps in, numbs the gut pain. Cori's heart beats.

A small ray slips away from the procession, a pup, maybe five meters across. It flaps up the slope—a flickering of gold and winking stars. It halts, hovers a half-dozen paces away from me, sways in the morning sun. The amber discs on the flat angled face flit back and forth; to Kibo, to me, to him, to me. We see eye to curious eye. Golden pupils within black irises within discs of amber. A huff like muffled thunder rises from the valley. The pup snaps its wings, flips up and over, then pirouettes and sideslips back down the slope. It merges back into the procession.

Down the valley a pair of golden rays, their trident tails flicking, flashing, mark the procession's end.

Morning sun warms the back of my neck.

"Cori. Look," I murmur. "Remember…"

A silent heart. A silent breath. Glittering ghosts…sighing…into a breathless… golden…haze.

The Thin Rising Line

Kiran Kaur Saini

"The Thin Rising Line" is original to *Bullet Points*, and it jumps off the page. It is a touching family story set in a society that takes the idea of a citizen militia to sadistic levels. Kiran Kaur Saini's stories have appeared in *Strange Horizons*, the *Magazine of Fantasy & Science Fiction*, *Gulf Coast*, and elsewhere. At the start of the pandemic, she left fifteen years in film production to care for her 89-year-old mom. In her spare time she practices Szymanowski and Mompou preludes on her family's 1927 reproducing piano. Find Kiran on Twitter @KirSphere.

THE TEXT CAME JUST as Jani left the locker room for hockey practice. "I'm out front in the car. The inspector's coming early. You have to come home right now."

JANI PUNCHED AT THE phone with her thumbs. "I just laced up my skates!"

"Sorry, hon," her mom texted back.

They drilled the procedure in the car. There were four in the family and each had to know not only their own role but also everyone else's, just in case.

"Are we in trouble?" Jani asked. "Did they find out we don't keep it mounted?"

Her mom shook her head. "It sounded like somebody dropped out of the program. We got moved up."

"You can drop out of the program?"

"Well…" Her mother looked troubled. "I don't think it's a straightforward process."

Jani mulled this over.

They had only an hour before the inspector arrived. Dad and Robbi were already lugging the weapon out of the basement. Mom started pushing the furniture to the sides and Jani rolled the dropcloth out. In the event that the inspector wanted to see the weapon discharged, the steel mesh would prevent potential carpet burns. The living room was built for this, but the rug was non-standard. Dad set the tripod down in the middle and Robbi ran the microfiber cloth over the parts so no dust would reveal their neglect. He touched the metal with the back of his hand. "It's cold. He'll know we had it in the basement."

Mom checked her watch. "I think we'll be okay." She yanked the curtains back. "We'll let the sun hit it."

Soon the household was filled with nothing but the hum of concentration and the ratcheting sounds of metal components sliding into place. The family worked together like a surgical team, outstretched hands filling with needed parts or tools without a word spoken.

At the appointed time, Jani and Dad peeled off to retrieve the financial records and put them on the coffee table.

The final assembly snapped into place. Dad clicked his stopwatch. "Boo yah. We've still got it."

When the doorbell rang the family was draped around the living room in relaxed poses, Dad tinkering with a broken clock, Mom and Robbi bent together over Robbi's chessboard, Jani reading this month's *Ammo*.

Mom brought the inspector into the living room. He sized up the weapon, nodded in appreciation, and rubbed his hands together. "Okay, let's see whatcha got."

Each of the kids had to load the weapon by themselves in the time allotted without prompting from their parents. Then they verbally walked the inspector through the weapon's disassembly and reassembly, never letting on that they'd just reassembled the weapon for the first time in months just half an hour ago.

The inspector quizzed them on the firing statistics of the weapon, asked for suggestions of similar launchers in the event that this one were unavailable or decommissioned, and listened to their prepared speeches on the efficacy and necessity of the Family Individual Defense Act. Jani and Robbi both passed with flying colors.

The inspector relaxed into their couch and swiped through the family's maintenance records, ammunition purchases, and range documentation. "It seems you missed a day at the practice range in June."

"That was the opening of the summer art show." Mom said. "Robbi had a painting accepted and we all went to the reception." Robbi pointed to a painting on the forward wall. There was the family's previous issue, a Gatling GshG 7.62, depicted in loose brush strokes that captured the essential nature and gestural movement of the weapon without being too literal. Spanky, the family dog, was portrayed curling around the base of the tripod as around the legs of a beloved master.

"Nice," the inspector nodded.

Finally, he flipped through their bank accounts and income statements, his feet up on their coffee table. At the end of his survey, he snapped the computer shut and swung his feet back to the ground.

"Everything appears in good order," he said. "Let's just run the test, shall we?"

Mom slid the living room window open.

The inspector went to the weapon and spun the controls until it pointed toward the ceiling.

"Let's have"—he consulted his notes—"Jani do it."

Jani stepped forward, sweat forming on her fingers. She hadn't been asked to fire the launcher in two years, and although she and Mom had run through the coordinates in the car, she still felt the pressure of the consequences if she made a mistake. The inspector started his timer.

Hands shaking, Jani whispered the positions to herself as she made each adjustment. Was she remembering correctly? It was harder to think when the weapon was live and the inspector was watching. The test field was 7.2 miles away, tucked between two residential neighborhoods, a shopping mall, and the rival high school that Jani's team had beat Saturday night in their last hockey match. Jani had to line the machine up without consulting any maps.

"Ten seconds," the inspector said. Everyone stepped toward the sides of the room.

Jani twirled levers, checked angles, the smooth, oily dials resisting her grip. "Done!"

"Deploy," the inspector said.

Jani paused.

"Deploy! Deploy!" the inspector shouted. "You have 1.5 seconds!"

Jani deployed.

Fire engulfed the back of the room and flared out, laying down another petal of the dark flower blossoming on the reinforced back wall. The missile catapulted out of the living room and sailed across the street, over the neighbor's house where Mr. Peterson stood watering his lawn. He looked up, then gave them a wave. The family watched in silence as the projectile coasted beyond the neighborhood and out of sight.

They waited.

At last a muffled detonation rumbled through the ground and they stared out the window, waiting for the thin rising line that would appear in the distant sky over the impact.

The inspector's phone rang. He picked it up, listened. "Understood." He clicked it off, turned to Jani. "Good job, kid. Right on target."

Jani exhaled. She hadn't realized she'd been holding her breath.

The inspector stood up and pulled a brochure out of his pocket. "The new equipment for next year. Here's the acquisition timeline, payment plan." He tossed it onto the coffee table.

Jani's dad snatched it up, flipped through. "We can't afford this. We just finished paying off this one."

The inspector turned back to the family, eyebrow raised, and gave a simple glance from parents to kids. "Neither of these skippers has an after school job, I saw."

"Yes, but they're..." Jani's mom started, but stopped. She looked at the inspector, eyes and unspoken words filled with Jani and Robbi's dreams.

"Actually," Jani piped up, "we're leaving the program."

"What are you talking about?" the inspector said.

Jani's parents shook their heads, but Jani ignored them. "The program," she repeated. "We're dropping out."

The inspector broke into a smile and rubbed Jani's arm. "No, no, sweetie, you did fine."

"What do you mean?" Jani asked.

"You passed. You hit the target. You won't be dropped from the program."

"I'm saying we *want* to leave the program," Jani said. "If the family before us quit, we can, too."

The inspector laughed. "Oh, honey, they didn't quit. They missed the target. Took out a whole block of a housing development in the Southwestern District. 600 souls. They're definitely... out. But you"—he patted her shoulder—"you guys are a genuine asset, the real deal. You got nothing to worry about."

As the inspector drove his van out of the cul-de-sac, Jani's mom slid the living room window shut.

"Don't worry," Jani's dad said. "We'll figure something out."

He and Robbi were already disassembling the weapon and starting to carry its parts back to the basement where they wouldn't have to see it for the next six months. Or maybe, with the new requirements, maybe it would just stay down there indefinitely. While the family acquired and struggled to learn the new issue, something bigger and better, this one would remain with the family's previous issues, all seventeen of them, lined up in the basement, waiting for the danger to come.

Merry-Go-Round

Liam Hogan

Liam Hogan is an award-winning short story writer, with stories in *Best of British Science Fiction* and *Best of British Fantasy* (NewCon Press). He's been published by *Analog*, *Daily Science Fiction*, and Flame Tree Press, among others. He helps host Liars' League London, volunteers at the creative writing charity Ministry of Stories, and lives and avoids work in London. "Merry-Go-Round" shows how strategic decisions about war affect individual experiences in warfare. This story is original to *Bullet Points*.

S O YOU GET TO Alteron first," the grease monkey said, yanking the straps that held me securely within the needle-nosed fighter, "which means you'll land *last*."

"HUH? WAIT, WHAT?"

She grinned. Short hair, freckles—or oil splatters? Kind of cute, though insanely young. And all over me, at the moment, though purely from a *professional* perspective.

"Weren't paying attention during briefing, were you, flyboy?"

I bristled and probably blushed. She waved it away.

"Don't worry, it happens, 'specially for virgins."

I didn't think I could *get* any redder.

"The *Goliath* has only just begun her descent," she went on. "Turned ass over tit, engines toward our destination, slowing us down. You're in the first wave of fighters—the shock wave. And once we kick you overboard, you're *NOT* slowing.

"Meaning you'll hit Alteron traveling at something like thirty thousand kilometers a second. Initial reports suggest Alteron's defense system extends maybe thirty-five k-klicks—as far out as geostat. So your war will be over in just over two seconds from first contact."

I knew all *that*. Knew the targeting systems would have already selected things for my missiles to hit. And for 'missiles' read chunks of depleted uranium—when you're traveling at a tenth of *c* you *are* the missile. Best we could do is give them a little nudge so they fanned out onto the right trajectory, though like the drones that preceded me, I'd be beaming back valuable intel for the next, somewhat slower, more precise wave.

I was there, as human pilot, because tactical AIs had calculated we gave a small but appreciable advantage in making any final decisions when there were a lot of targets in the sector. The squadron had trained hard for this. For our month of complete and utter boredom, speeding along on near-starvation rations, muscles wasting away in zero-g and tubes going places it wouldn't be polite to mention, followed by about an hour of final approach planning, and then weapons hot and heavy and *blam*!

I still didn't get it, the landing last bit. Maybe *I* was the monkey, like those dumb animals first sent into space in the way-back-when.

"So you exit the battle stage right, and you're *still* going thirty thousand kilometers an hour," she patiently explained. "Heading *away* from Alteron."

"Oh." The penny finally dropped. "And then I start decelerating?"

She laughed. *Actually* laughed. "You see any fuel tanks on this heap of junk?"

I had to admit I didn't. I squinted at the area above her left breast, trying to read the name badge without appearing to lech.

"You and you alone, in the tiny support pod which is this cockpit, will get thrown out and back from your speeding fighter at as many G as you can handle and fly by the fifth planet, the gas giant, close enough to shoot turkeys, all to put you into an extreme elliptical orbit, *still* heading away. Then you go to sleep, gravity does its thing and the *Goliath* mops up. We come pick you up on your way back into the inner system. Assuming," she went on, the pink tip of her tongue poking out as she checked my life support stats, "I've cinched the straps tight enough and you're not instant jelly."

She looked me in the eye. Scanned them, searching for something, perhaps. Nodded. "Don't worry, all that stuff is automatic which is why you haven't had to do it in the simulator over and over. You'll be *fine*. Just better hope the war is a short one and you don't have to go around *twice*."

I blinked and she laughed again.

"*Joking.* Long as you don't hit anything on the way through. Though your relative speed means even if that *anything* is stood still it's still going to…ah, no point in getting all graphic. If you get to the deep sleep stage, you're *golden*. Unless we actually lose the war," she chuckled, as if that was an impossibility, "we'll be picking you flyby heroes up and for you it'll be like an hour has gone by."

I finally twigged what the most important question was. "And for the *Goliath*? How long for you?"

She smiled. "'Bout twelve years. The age gap between us won't exist any more. I might even outrank you." She looked me up and down, trussed as I was, the neck and head brace meaning I couldn't look anywhere else except those steady hazel eyes. "You can maybe buy me a drink, for rescuing your ass?"

I smiled back. "I'd be delighted, *Lieutenant Elena Rodriguez*."

C APTAIN MACKENSIE MOSEYED OVER while the prepped fighter was being wheeled toward the carrier deck.

"You do your usual thing, Roddy?"

She watched the needle jet exit the cavernous hanger before turning to her boss. "If you mean give him a reason to live, then yes."

"And how many fighters have you dispatched these last two weeks?"

She reddened. "Eighteen."

"Going to be a full dance card."

She turned on the captain, a flash of anger in her eyes, but only for a moment. War was hell, and she—they—were only doing what was necessary. "The other engineers, they tell the truth?"

It was his turn to look sheepish. "Don't suppose they do. What did you make it? Twelve years?"

"Long enough to be remarkable, short enough not to scare the bejesus out of them. Don't suppose we'd get many volunteers if they knew."

"You'd be surprised." The captain shook his head. "We keep 'em separate from the grunts, but we've got some veterans on this mission."

"Oh? How many times?"

"Five, one of them. This'll be their number six."

"Six rides on the ol' merry-go-round? Is he some sort of dinosaur?"

"*She*. And yes. But she says she's getting to see the universe—change. Always something new and interesting to wake up to. Plus, she outlives *all* her exes."

Six times two centuries…A twelve hundred-year-old soldier? Roddy shuddered. It didn't bear thinking about.

Read *Rise of Ahrik*, the gripping military science fiction epic in the tradition of Frank Herbert and Orson Scott Card. Ahrik's journey will draw you in as he fights to save the world.

Artist Known

Caias Ward

"Artist Known" originally appeared in *Daily Science Fiction*. This story captures the power of a relationship between a mother and child to transcend war and memory. Caias Ward is a thick-wristed HVAC technician with over two dozen publication credits. A member of the Science Fiction and Fantasy Writers Association and Codex Writers, he currently lives with his wife and daughter in New Jersey, where he enjoys terrible movies and agitating for labor. Find him @caias on Twitter and @CaiasWard@wandering.shop on Mastodon.

WE KNOW WE LOST the war, a war based around what would be considered "reality," by seeing a history which isn't ours.

THE TALLARIAN EMPIRE NO longer is; it never was. I do not know what is this "Rome," or why we have a Gregorian calendar instead of the Daystar's Ascension calendar. My familiar candy bars, the PimPam and the Hoostaloo Bites, are replaced with "Snickers" and "Kit-Kats." I do not know many things, and my stolen neural catalog shows me an alternate reality which is all too real now. They changed enough things in time and space, altered enough of the past and present and future, that we can't hope to restore it.

My daughter no longer is.

I mean, I remember her, for now. But as changes in time ripple through and the fabric of reality sets, I forget. I had a wife. I know I had a wife, but I know nothing of how we met. I do not remember who was pregnant with our daughter, me or her. I don't remember my daughter's name. But they can't get rid of everything. No matter how much they strike, what events they bleach and redye, the fabric of reality stains with What Was Before. Even their temporal bleaching and dyeing of the spacetime fabric leaves the threads weak and bare.

And in this weakness, I will force reality to remember my daughter even after I am bleached away.

I'm near a museum. Museums are secondary battlegrounds in the war. Here, even as history of the past and the future changes, not everything gets bleached perfectly clean. Objects which defy the past they make still stain the fabric of the world. Sometimes the enemy has to accept that some stains will stick, unless they are willing to cut away even more reality and unravel even more spacetime. We hide in trenches cut up and down spacetime, in tiny redoubts of parallel dimension. Here, we wait to go over the top and be unraveled as the threads of our being are pulled to satisfy the new reality, all so we can grab a few more feet of history. In this trench of a garden apartment nearby, multiple Mes and others time-traveled from various points, crammed in and planning and waiting. The Oldest among us are nervous there is no one Older than them still. The Youngers are terrified that they will become the broken threadbare phantoms the Olders are, or simply disappear when the changes in reality become too much. All from our side know we have lost.

We fight not for our history, but for memory now. A beloved place here, a cherished name there. All things that an enemy we never wanted to make and don't even know are trying to erase, paint over, dye. All to get the reality *they* want with the places and people and names they want. Those places and people and names don't include us, so into the bleach we go.

I fight for a bauble, a bit of spun blue glass. In my daughter's apprenticeship, she heated the glass, drew it out into a spiral, careful, careful…and she wrapped leather around it and tied a cord to it. It was apprentice work. It was not her greatest work; *that* glorious piece of shimmering colors rested in the Ceberian Trust when such a place existed in spacetime. It was not her most expensive work, which sold at auction for nineteen million *votens*. But this spun blue glass bauble was her most important work, because she gave it to me as a gift and it is the last piece of her art which exists in reality.

It is pretty, pretty as her smile.

I remember my daughter's smile, and I confirm by asking the others of Me present; most

remember it. She had blue lips from the azomeberries she would eat constantly. Those berries don't exist anymore/never existed. But I remember the smile and her blue crooked incisor. I remember how she would hold the glass bauble up to the light and paint the wall with blue, dance it about for me and my…

I had a wife. We had a daughter. I do not remember which one of us carried our daughter. They both do not exist any longer.

If I succeed in this mission, a glass bauble of spun blue will hang in a museum display, missed or reluctantly accepted by those who are bleaching away my reality in favor of theirs. Someone will walk in that museum one day and light will strike the glass *just so*. Color will paint their eyes with inspiration. They will carry that home and create something, something flashed with blue light. Paintings of lakes. Incredible dresses of cerulean silks. Songs full of serenity, courage, and wisdom.

In my trench in spacetime, I look to the other Mes. They are scared, trembling. Some are angry. Some I remember being, and others I do not. When you fight this much in time and space, people fray too. We are so frayed, threads plucked and washed out and ripped, like how Zhara would tear her wedding dress each day to avoid marrying Ilther.

I see no other Me who is older.

I hold up my bauble to the wan ceiling lamp to paint each of us blue. The others do the same. The light is cool on us. For a moment, we are blue with peace. For a moment, we know our daughter exists, regardless of what reality says.

We trade baubles around. The mismatch of baubles and owners will strain spacetime and one bauble might stick. Again, too much bleach, you can wreck the fabric. They might just have to leave it rather than risk an unraveling of reality.

After the war, someone will look at that bauble, see a description on a card.

Blue glass pendant. Artist unknown.
Reality will know her, though.

Spun Yarn

RAY DALEY

Ray Daley was born in Coventry and still lives there. He served six years in the Royal Air Force as a clerk and spent most of his time in a Hobbit hole in High Wycombe. He is a published poet and has been writing stories since he was 10. His current dream is to eventually finish the *Hitch Hikers* fanfic novel he's been writing since 1986. Tweet him @RayDaleyWriter. "Spun Yarn" is original to *Bullet Points*. The use of exquisite British idioms and spelling in this story is deliberate. Reader reflections on the power of perception in war are also intentional.

MY LEG WAS FEELING a lot better today. I was able to walk to sick parade. Only needed one crutch too. We had a new medical officer this morning. Barely old enough to be shaving, from the number of cuts on his face. *Physician, heal thyself!* Poor bugger. It took all my self control to not laugh while he was asking me how I felt.

"JIMISIN?"

I did my best to stand to attention, tough with the gimpy leg and a crutch. "Sir!"

He looked me up and down. His eyes immediately caught the shorts. "Aren't you out of uniform, man?"

I shook my head, flashing him my sick chit, "Excused trousers, sir, on account of the leg wound. The trouser legs rather do press on the bandages. Previous MO said it might lead to blood clots, so he wrote me a chit. The shorts are uniform, sir. PT kit. Standard issue."

He looked down at my records. "The sheet says ... "

That was my cue to fill in the blanks. "Shrapnel, right leg, between the knee and ankle, sir. I know. The field medic was a tad rushed, on account of how we were taking heavy enemy fire at the time. I'm sorry you can't read his writing."

The baby medic raised an eyebrow. "Is there blood on this form, Jimisin?"

I nodded. "That'd be mine, sir. Your finest line in Terran O Positive, sir."

I could see the bile rising in his throat. Ah, one of those, eh? Fresh out of med school, as yet unsullied by the horrors of war. *Lucky bastard.* "I was told by the previous incumbent the new forms were on backorder, sir. I'll help you fill it out when they arrive. And I'll try not to get any of my blood on it this time. Should be a lot easier, back here, away from the front."

He swallowed, failing to make it obvious he'd just sicked up into his mouth. "Okay then, Jimisin, if you can keep still, I'll take a shufti." He unrolled the bandages. Considering how deep the wound had been, he did well not to puke his guts out when he saw it. He had to take a good deep breath to stop himself though. "Phew. This is a nasty one, and no mistake. Keep applying the antibacterial cream, let the wound air for an hour each day. Are you seeing the nurse?"

I nodded. "Yes, sir. We're scheduled for daily visits."

"Let her know to double your medication dosage. No bloody point writing it here. Was there anything else?"

Bloody hell. He was green. Didn't even know the sick parade drill yet! I tried not to eyeball him. "You're supposed to make a decision if I'm fit to return to full active duty or not, sir. You know, I've got to get back to killing those heartless alien bastards." I decided against telling him he was supposed to replace the dressing himself. I'd do it once he dismissed me.

Speaking of which…

I could see him running down a mental checklist as he looked at me. His eyes were literally flicking from left to right, as he was ticking off items, reaching a diagnosis. "As the wound is still deep and open, it wouldn't be a good idea to return you to the field yet. We'll keep you here for another month, I think. No need to attend daily sick parades either, take this chit. Excused

sick parade for the next month, by order of the Chief Medical Officer. Are we done here, then?"

I smiled. "Not allowed to leave until officially dismissed by an officer, sir."

"Very well, Jimisin. You're dismissed. Go on then, bugger off."

I hobbled far enough away on my crutch as to be out of his immediate field of view. I reached the bench at the base of the Observation Tower and quickly rewrapped the dressing around my leg once again. While it had been nice to feel the breeze on my skin, I knew I had to keep it covered if I wanted to carry on using that leg. *Or have any hope of not losing it.*

I didn't really need to rest, but I had nothing better to do, so I took in the air. In hindsight, I should have gone back to the ward. Or to the library. Or anywhere which wasn't that particular bench.

I might have avoided a conversation with the Discip Sergeant then. "That man on the bench! Stand to attention!"

As I sat up, I pulled out one of my sick chits. "All due respect, Sergeant, I can't. Leg wound. I've got a chit."

He marched himself up to the bench, slamming his boots into the ground as he halted in front of me. He snatched the piece of paper from my hand. "Give me that. Bloody malingerers!"

I waited while he read the thing, then allowed his face to reset. "Ah, sorry, son. Wounded by heavy fire whilst rescuing another man. Didn't realise. Have they recommended you for the combat honour medal yet? If not, I'd be happy to nominate you myself?"

I let him squirm for a few minutes while I remained silent. "Sergeant! Didn't see you there! Just give me a minute to stand to attention!"

He waved me away. "You stay sat down, lad, after all, you've got this." He handed my chit back to me.

My acting was better than his. "Excused standing to attention for a leg wound? When did that happen, Sarge? I don't recall things all too well any more…"

I could see he was starting to get uncomfortable now. Perfect. That was exactly how he usually made us feel. "Listen, son, if you like, I'll call for an orderly to help you back to your ward?"

I waved him off. "No, Sarge, it's fine. I can walk. Just need to catch my breath, gather my thoughts. You know how it is, man with your level of experience."

I'd kicked him right in the ego there. He hadn't seen any combat yet, and nor was he likely to, either. Not unless he was the last man left in our army. "You relax there, lad. I'll see to it that no-one bothers you. Take a nap, if you need one. You won't be disturbed."

He marched off swiftly, before I could damage his ego any further.

I was almost surprised. Most of the others who hadn't seen combat always asked me what it had been like. I normally gave them the same answer. We never saw hide nor hair of the enemy, but the brass always told us how terrible they were. How they invaded local villages, killing their women and children. It was always the same stories, the enemy were inhuman, they had no feelings, how utterly alien to us they were.

AS PLEASANT AS IT was to not have to attend the daily sick parade, I got an odd level of enjoyment out of the morning hobble there and back. I got bored of not going, over that month off.

When the time came, I was okay with being told to report for sick parade again.

One of the orderlies woke me from a nap to pass on the message. "Gunner Jimisin? You'll be required to attend sick parade tomorrow. Just so you know, it's held on the main parade square now. Report at oh nine hundred hours. Understood?"

I spent the day making sure my green shirt and battledress were well ironed, and in a good presentable order.

That morning, most of us were there at least ten minutes early, idly shooting the shit, swapping horror stories of how we'd been injured. We were the lucky ones though, the walking wounded. I'd heard about those far worse off than us, the basket-cases up on the top floor. Then the Discip Sergeant marched onto the parade square, slamming to a halt in front of us.

"Okay then, my boys. If we can make a nice straight line, that would make me a very happy Sergeant. Can you do that for me, lads?"

It took us the rest of the eight minutes we had left to get ourselves into any semblance of a formation for him, but we managed it, barely.

I could have sworn he almost had a tear in his eye as he marched down our rank. "Wonderful, wonderful. Done me proud, you have. Okay. The new CMO is on his way. Stand to attention, if you can. If you can't, just stand as smartly as you're able to."

As we stood there, a new officer started marching down the line. "Okay, listen in, gentlemen. If I call your name, take one step forward. I understand that might be difficult for some of you, just do your best, take as long as you need." Then he started calling names off the clipboard he was carrying. Until he got to me. "Jimisin!"

Little did I know that by stepping forward, I had just volunteered myself for an as yet unknown duty.

THE LAST THING I remember clearly was being asked to go to the orderly room for a vitamin injection. Then I guess I fell asleep? I hadn't felt that tired, but when you're wounded, the body tends to take care of itself. If you need rest, you sleep. Quite often, the brain has no say in the matter.

Opening my eyes, I examined my surroundings. I wasn't back in the ward.

It looked like one of our aid centres. Had they decided I wasn't serious enough to stay in hospital any longer then? They'd moved me to an aid station so I could be closer to the front when I had recovered enough to return to active duty? I wasn't about to assume anything, yet.

"Gunner Jimisin, is it?"

I nodded. He was wearing the familiar orderly uniform. No rank insignia of any kind though. I filed that under unusual.

"Yes. Sorry, I can't see any rank. What do I call you?"

He smiled. It felt relaxing. "Well, my name's Hampton. You can call me that, if you like?"

I still felt slightly uneasy. "The thing is, I'm a soldier. I'm used to addressing people by their rank. It's my leg that was injured, not my personality. Are you not a soldier then?"

Hampton shook his head. "I can understand your concern. I'm a civilian volunteer. We don't have ranks. Though if you need a title, you can always call me 'Orderly.' That's what I am, not who I am. I'd prefer Hampton, personally, but it's entirely up to you. I'm afraid we didn't receive any paperwork on you. Could I ask your first name?"

"Sure. Millis. M. I. Double L. I. S. Yes, it is an unusual name. From my paternal grandfather, I was given to understand."

Hampton was a nice enough guy. He read to me, brought me meals, and reassured me when we received incoming fire.

My days were comfortable. Unless we were being bombed, that was. My time was my own, my leg was getting better much sooner than the hospital had anticipated.

And that view. What an amazing view. *Of the Observation Tower.*

IT TOOK ME A few days to process that. *I could see the Observation Tower.*

It was four days before I decided to ask Hampton about that.

"I'm afraid it's Olusioun soup again today, sorry about that Millis. I've added extra chives; I know you like those."

I looked up from the cot. "Hampton, if I asked you a question, would you promise to answer truthfully?"

He smiled, placing the bowl of soup on the floor beside me. "Sure, ask anything."

"I noticed the view outside yesterday. It's a breath-taking vantage. Of the allied Observation Tower."

He nodded. "Yes, we're extremely lucky here. It's quite the outlook, isn't it?"

I rubbed my hand across my face. I'd have to spell it out for him, it seemed. "Hampton, old friend. There's realistically only one location I could have such a great view of that tower. And that'd be from anywhere within Hermian territory. I'm behind bloody enemy lines, aren't I?"

Hampton brushed down his white tunic. "Millis. You were quite seriously injured in the bombing, you know that?"

I'd taken a bad shrapnel hit. Deep, but not what I'd have called life threatening. I rolled the blanket off my body. While I'd been sleeping, someone had dressed me. *In a Hermian uniform.* I looked up at him. "What happened to my green battledress, Hampton? I'll be shot as a spy, if I'm found wearing this."

To his credit, Hampton's smile never dropped a millimetre. "Come on now, Millis. You know as well as I do, they don't shoot civilians."

I gave him a hard stare. "It's Gunner Jimisin. Serial number—"

He stopped me before I had a chance to rattle it off. "I know, Millis. That's the cover story. It looks like our deep programming works too. You know as well as I do that the enemy treats prisoners, but only military prisoners. They don't understand how we live. We don't want a war. We didn't even have a fighting force, until the darn Terrans invaded. Hermia is a peaceful world. We asked the Terrans to leave us alone. We seceded from their governorship over a thousand years ago. Most people on Hermia don't even know what a Terran even looks like any more. Speaking of which ... How did the intelligence gathering mission go? You must feel a lot better now, out of that awful Terran uniform?"

I just lay there, looking at him, utterly dumbfounded. "But…but…the Hermians are the enemy. They kill women and children. They raze entire settlements. They're a heartless, cold, alien race. Hampton."

He started to shake his head. "Oh, my word. That deep programming might have been a little too much, especially after the shell shock. Don't worry, Millis. We placed you in the crater with the dying Terran officer. I still remember what he said to me as we put you there. 'You bloody noncoms, you all look alike to me. Thanks for saving my life though, I'll see you get a medal for this.' Of course we had to dress you in a uniform, so they'd take you back and treat you. Did they not mention the prisoner exchange before you came back then? I think you'd better come with me."

He helped me out of the cot, and we made our way out of the tent to a small prefab building a few steps away. Inside, it was all so far removed from the battlefield. Clean, clinical, the latest equipment. Even the paint was still wet.

"In here, Millis."

Here was a large medical scanner. So new, Hampton had to tear film covers off the control panels. "If you sit there, I'll check what those bloody Terrans got up to in that head of yours."

I WANT TO SAY it felt like a dream, being with the Terrans. More like a nightmare, now I've had the barriers lifted from my mind. We have seen the enemy, and they are us. Not like us, they *are* us. Or at least they used to be.

"They lie to their men, Hampton. Such mistruths. They call us monsters, accuse us of foul deeds. All lies. They have no idea they're fighting other human beings, Hampton. How do you defeat an enemy like that?"

He rolled the bandages back. The flesh was almost entirely healed. "Another week here, I think. Then we'll find that green battledress for you again. Do you think you can remember your medical training? You did say the hospital had a heavy turnover of medical officers, after all. All those wounded men, I'd wager they'll listen to a Doctor, won't they? They can tell stories? We've got stories they won't believe. I'll get you started in the deep programming room in the morning. Key phrase?"

"Once upon a time, a thousand years ago, on a planet called Hermia…"

The Compulsion of Venus

C. B. DROEGE

C. B. Droege is an author and voice actor from the Queen City living in the Millionendorf. His writing influences include Philip K. Dick, Bill Bryson, Isaac Asimov, David Sedaris, and Roger Zelazny. He loves wizards and time-travel, but has an irrational distaste for time-traveling wizards. His latest books are *Ichabod Crane and the Magic Lamp and Other Stories* and *Quantum Age Adventures*. Short fiction publications include work in *Nature Futures*, *Daily Science Fiction*, and dozens of other magazines and anthologies. He also produces a weekly podcast, in which he reads other people's stories: *Manawaker Studio's Flash Fiction Podcast*. "The Compulsion of Venus" is original to *Bullet Points*, with whispers of Thucydides' Melian Dialogue.

IN THE HEART OF the Venusberg Capitol Complex, Chairman Lee of the Sol Council stared, half-lidded, across a table of polished Venusian obsidian. He'd lost his posture over the last hour of conversation, and was nearly sliding out of the armchair. He maintained this pose for a full minute of silence, then abruptly drew in a breath, drummed his fingers noiselessly on the table.

"ARE YOU TELLING ME that after more than two centuries of enjoying the benefits of the Rampion Accord, your people intend to not keep their end of the deal?"

"No," Governor Boris Journo sighed and pinched the bridge of his nose, feeling as though he'd explained this enough already. "I'm saying that the terms don't apply."

"The language is very clear," the chairman said, abruptly regaining his posture. "In the event of a military need, The Venusian government will supply a military force equal to five percent of their adult population. There is not much ambiguity."

Boris took a deep breath and raised his eyes to look at the chairman, who emanated an intimidating aura, all calm confidence and resolve. "The Rampion accords were signed in a very different time." He tried to keep his voice steady. "Two centuries ago, humans still thought they were alone in the universe, and they certainly had no concept of The Menace or the threat they present."

"You admit then, that The Menace represents a threat to humanity that cannot be ignored?" the chairman asked.

Boris ignored the question. "Further, Venus' population at that time only consisted of a few thousand people, mostly soldiers and scientists, on one poorly maintained orbital and a tiny surface colony. The dozens of aerostat colonies and millions of *free* residents of Venus weren't even a dream to those men. They were still rebuilding from the ATaPH attack and the Battle for Sovereignty. Sam Rampion Jr. may have written the accords, and signed them on our behalf, but there was no way for any of those men to know what would become of Venus over the years."

The chairman slid down a bit into the chair again, resting one elbow on the smooth dark red stone. He spoke as if explaining to a grade school classroom. "If every contract and treaty could be broken just because circumstances change, then there would be no need to ever make such agreements. The point is that you must hold up your end, even if it is unpleasant for you."

"Unpleasant?" Boris tried to sound indignant, but felt like he probably just sounded shrill. "Chairman, our military forces currently only equal two percent of our adult population, which is already twice the rate of the rest of the Human Alliance. If we were to fulfill this demand, we'd have to conscript over a hundred thousand men and women. It's impossible. It's unfair. Conscription hasn't been practiced in any human culture since before Terran Unification. Venus is willing to turn its entire military force over to Sol command for the duration of the threat. That must be enough!"

It was the chairman's turn to sigh. He stood and walked casually over to the large window behind his chair, looking out over the Capitol Gardens. "It's too bad," he said, voice so low that Boris had to strain to hear, "that Sam Rampion Jr. and his compatriots didn't just join the new Sol Council all those years ago. Things would be much simpler now, wouldn't they?"

"Perhaps," Boris said slowly, "but the past is in the past, chairman."

"You know"—Chairman Lee turned back to face the governor, as if he'd had a sudden idea; it was an obvious contrivance—"It's not too late to correct their mistake."

"What do you mean?" Boris narrowed his eyes. He did not like where this was going.

"Bring Venus fully into the Sol Council now," the chairman said, "then Venus and its citizens would be protected by all the same rights and provisions that protect every other human in the galaxy, and they would no longer be bound by the Rampion Accord."

None of the previous officials to visit regarding this issue had taken it in this direction. "That option is not on the table," Boris said. "The Venusian people value their independence from the Sol Council. Even if I considered it an option, they would never stand for it."

The chairman gave his best, well-practiced frown. "That's too bad. So much unpleasantness could be avoided."

"Is that what all of this has been about?" Boris asked. "Have you been pushing this issue for so long so that you can use it as a threat against us, an attempt to get us to capitulate to the rule of the Sol Council?"

"Of course not," the chairman said. "It was just a suggestion." There was a long pause between the men before Chairman Lee continued. "The Council would be happy to help with conscription efforts. We've got ships and soldiers standing by near Venusberg and each of the aerostat cities. On my word they will set up registration and recruitment centers, and begin a conscription lottery. It would only take a few months to help you get to the numbers required, and the Council is even willing to take up all incurred expenses for the process."

As the chairman spoke, Boris boiled. By the time the chairman was done, Boris' anger had settled into a cold hatred. He was starting to understand how Rampion and his followers must have felt two hundred and six years earlier, when the Sol Council brought their full weight down upon Venusberg. Suddenly, he understood why men went to war.

"The people will resist you," Boris said. "They will not volunteer, and they will not come when called. They will fight you in the corridors before they allow themselves to be forced into service."

"For everyone's sake, Governor Journo," the chairman said, coolly, "I hope you are wrong." Then he stood for a quiet few minutes. Boris got the impression that the chairman was waiting for something, but whatever it was, it never came, and the leader of the Sol Council swept from the room without another word.

Boris stared out the window for a long moment, wondering if this was the end of something, or the beginning of something. Then he put the thought out of his mind and called a special session of his cabinet and military advisors. They would need to begin preparations for whatever was to come.

We'll Make Them Pay

Daniel Crow

"We'll Make Them Pay" is original to *Bullet Points*, and offers a cautionary tale on the so-called cycle of violence. Does violence take on a life of its own, or do we have agency over war? Daniel Crow is a Russian-Israeli journalist and public relations associate living in Tel Aviv-Jaffa. Having grown up on Tolkien and Stephen King, he has long been in love with writing and all things fictional and grim, drawing inspiration from myths and folk tales of the past. His other passions include high-tech, history, and old comedy movies. His previous work has appeared in *Allegory*, *Metastellar*, and various anthologies.

THE SMUGGLERS NEVER SAW us coming. We approached silently, hiding in the tall grass, and fell upon them with our swords drawn. The seals of the Divine Mandate engraved upon cold steel in our hands glimmered in the sunlight as we made short work of their small squad. The fate of those who surrendered was sealed the moment we saw what they carried. Laser pistols were banned in the Valley, just like any other long-range weapon, even for border guards like us.

ANY FIREFIGHT COULD SET off a larger war, our leaders calculated, and a larger war was all but certain to see the treacherous Talganis fire their nuclear arsenal at our peace-loving people—a crime that could only be punished with a retaliatory strike.

"We keep the weapons," Captain Sword's Song ordered, pointing his metal finger at the payload. He lost his arm a month ago—a Talgani footman slashed it right off, cleanly and precisely. "We won't report them to observers and will carry them to next talks, concealed. If the Talgani scum try any tricks this time, we'll light them up."

I nodded and hurried to cover the antigrav-cart with camo cloth.

"We'll make them pay," I whispered, and the captain nodded silently.

WE WILL MEET FOR next de-escalation talks on this cliff," Captain Ashatari said, pointing at the holo-map of the Valley. He was of the noble caste, and his face had the same masculine beauty one would imagine ancient Talgani heroes to possess. "You will lead your men here, covered in camo-capes, up this trail, and prepare an ambush. Last month, they claimed three of our brothers. This month, we will have our revenge. Strike when you see us draw our steel."

The sergeant nodded. His own face was marked with a scar—he got it in the scuffle a couple moons ago, when the deceitful Sun Empire attacked his crew during the de-escalation talks.

The next morning, he led his men on the hidden trail up the cliff before spending hours in ambush. When he saw the captain draw his curved blade with a battlecry, he signaled his squad to attack. But as they charged at the enemy, the Sun soldiers met them with something they never expected: a volley of laser fire that melted armor and flesh alike. And as he fell on the ground, a charred hole smoldering in his chest, his last thought was, "We'll make them pay."

ON THE THIRTEENTH NIGHT of the cannonade, I had to send several soldiers, including my own brother Fading Sun, off to the medbay again. By that time, we had grown accustomed to the wailing of sirens and the rush to the shelters deep beneath our bunkers. But the shelling was still taking a toll, and not just on our bodies.

As the underground structures we were hiding in rocked so violently as if the sky itself was falling upon us, the weaker souls were reduced to whimpering and cries. Those were the ones I had to send off, those not strong enough to withstand this, night after night. I blamed none of them for their fear, though, for deep inside I also screamed every time a blast roared through the not-so-soundproof shelter, and the walls shook like crazy.

Only two thoughts helped me get through this, keeping myself together. One was that there, on the other edge of the Valley, the Taglani scum were similarly hunkering down in their own shelters as our long-range artillery blasted away at them from behind the mountain ridge.

My other thought was of the advance we will eventually mount, forward and down the rocky slopes, into the Valley, ours by right, yet claimed by the enemy. We'll come with laser rifles, not swords this time, and our weapons are already on the way here, with no observers to stop the shipments. I heard that the cargo was delayed, but they would come eventually. And when they finally arrive …

That's when we'll make the pay.

THIS IS THE LAST transmission we received from the capital." Captain Ashatri's voice was numb, and his gaze was dim as he looked at the screen. There was no sound in this video, which was probably for the better, for even silent, it got its message through in full.

Some of the men and women gathered in the underground hall wept when they saw the mushroom-like shapes rising over the beautiful city of glass and marble, while others stood silent, too shocked to even shed a tear. They watched the sky turn red before the video ended in a flurry of white noise.

"Tomorrow, our artillery will run out of shells," the captain said. "We expect the bastards to go empty by that time too. We are not aware of any incoming arms shipments, either for us or for them. I do not even know if the laser rifles are coming, and cannot reach out to anyone to confirm. But there is one thing I know for sure."

His eyes traveled along the room, looking everyone right into their souls—and setting those ablaze with its noble power and fury.

"We may very well be the last sons and daughters of the Talgani Communion standing," he said. "And tomorrow, when the big guns fall silent, we will march forth and cut down those bastards one by one. With our blades, we will cut, and slash, and chop until the last of them falls dead. No payment is large enough for what they did . . . And yet, tomorrow, we'll make them pay."

A T DAWN, GRIM AND gray, two battalions marched down either side of the Valley, ripped apart by the endless artillery strikes. Swords did not glimmer in their hands, as the sun was hidden behind the leaden clouds spewing radioactive rains, and grass did not rustle beneath their metal boots, as grass was no more. Many of them were limping, and the armor on some was all torn up and battered after being dug out of the rubble left by the shelling, and yet, they all marched side by side, silently, solemnly.

As they clashed, the Valley erupted with sound: with clinging of metal against metal, with screams and battle cries, with roaring and thunder. In the havoc of the fight, it was hard to tell who was the first to fall in the dirt and rubble beneath. It did not matter who fell and who remained standing anyway, for the sound that spelled the end for this cacophony was that of the radiation exposure trackers in their armor going crazy.

Within minutes, only the two captains were on their feet, their blades bloodied, their combat suits beaten and dented. They charged at each other and fought for another minute before one of them collapsed after a heavy blow. The other raised the hilt of his sword to the sky—the blade had shattered into pieces in the fight—and stood victorious for another heartbeat before falling onto the burnt rocks.

The echo of his fall rolled across the rubble, as loud as thunder . . . And then, the Valley was silent.

Ships Made of Guns

M. V. MELCER

M. V. Melcer is the author of forthcoming science fiction novel *Refractions* (November 2023). Her short fiction has appeared in *Clarkesworld*, *GigaNotoSurus*, *Nature*, and others. Born in Poland, M. V. lived in the United States, the Netherlands, and Belgium before settling in the United Kingdom. When not writing, she is pursuing a degree in astronomy. Find her at mvmelcer.com. "Ships Made of Guns" originally appeared in *Daily Science Fiction*. The twist at the end of this story buzzes with the frightful costs of war.

WHEN THE INVADERS APPEARED, I had no choice. I lowered my head and opened my arms to greet them. Some of us tried to fight, against my warnings, but the orbiting gunships put a quick end to the resistance. I made sure everyone learned the lesson: their ships are made of guns. You cannot stop them.

THEY SETTLED QUICKLY. THEY took what was ours and made it theirs. I served them well, and prospered. I offered them our secrets, revealed where the riches were hidden. People spat on me on the streets. I did not care. I was alive.

From my new mansion on the hill, I watched my world transformed. Slowly, the fires died, and ivy grew over the craters. In the ruins of the cities, I threw banquets to honor the oppressors.

Our masters rewarded good service. Citizens who didn't resist were set free. Soon the streets were busy again, even though the faces were tired and the backs hunched. I didn't care. We were alive.

And still some tried to fight. I helped track the rebellion. From my screen-lined office in planet security, I spoke to them: be wise. Stay alive. Their ships are made of guns. You cannot stop them.

The insurgents did not listen.

My reward was handsome. In my house, I covered all mirrors with black satin. No more would the traitor glare at me.

Soon gunships crowded the skies, each citizen's DNA tagged and tracked from orbit. My childhood friends conspired to sabotage the shipyard. I caught them in time. The guns fixed on their DNA, and they vanished.

I pulled down the satin and smashed all the mirrors till my fists bled. I didn't care. I was alive.

"Our ships are made of guns," the invaders said. "You cannot stop us."

They were wrong.

For I was alive. And I was waiting.

When their trust in me was complete, I was ready. Alone in the control room, I guided their flotilla of gunships. It'd taken months to alter the program, unnoticed; years to gather DNA imprints from remnants of my banquets. Now all I needed was the last, simple change.

I swapped our DNA markers with theirs. The computer hummed, and the guns retargeted.

This is the day of reckoning. My gun is made of their ships. They cannot stop me.

War Around the Clock

LARRY HODGES

"War Around the Clock" is original to *Bullet Points*, offering delicious strategic satire. Larry Hodges, from Germantown, Maryland, is an active member of the Science Fiction & Fantasy Writers Association (SFWA), with over 130 short story sales (over 170 with reprints) and four novels. He's a member of Codex Writers and a graduate of the Odyssey and the Taos Toolbox Writers Workshops. He has nineteen books and over 2,100 published articles in over 180 different publications. He's also a member of the USA Table Tennis Hall of Fame, and claims to be the best table tennis player in SFWA, and the best science fiction writer in USA Table Tennis!

THERE WAS ANOTHER STRAFING run and tank bombardment as they passed Twelve at midnight, and many soldiers were killed. But the short, heavyset General Shorthand, his skin as dark as the darkest coal, raised his sword grimly and cried, *"Onward!"*

THE ARMY MARCHED ON over the white expanse, curving to the right.

"If all goes well, we'll reach One in an hour," said the tall, balding Colonel, biting his nails. He was a veteran of many battles, with a missing right ear and left middle finger. He held his right hand over his head as if to protect his head from bullets. "But we can't take another strafing!"

"You always say that," said the General, returning Hickory to its scabbard. "Yet here we are."

"And here *they* are," said the Colonel. They'd been marching just over a minute and already the fighter jets were arcing overhead again, strafing them. *"Hit the dirt!"*

"Negative!" cried the General. "On your feet,

soldiers! Onward, always onward! Anyone stopping will face my sword!" The bullets smacked about them, and some fell, but the rest continued.

The soldiers fired their machine guns at the jets as they passed overhead and away. Every now and then they brought one down, but not this time.

The Colonel suddenly screamed as a bullet shot through his right arm, which exploded in blood and gore, leaving him with just a stump. As blood gushed out from around the exposed bone, he continued to march, stumbling a bit as he struggled to keep up.

"*Medic!*" cried the General. The medic cauterized and bandaged the Colonel's stump as they walked.

"You'll make it, I promise," said the General.

"Are you sure?" asked the Colonel, wincing, his face pale.

"I absolutely promise. Your bravery is noted. But keep moving—One is a highly strategic target." Then the General shook his head. "War is Hell."

"Here they come again!" cried the Colonel. Over and over they were strafed—sixty times the first hour. Many brave men and women lost their lives, but the infantry never slowed their pace.

"There it is!" the Colonel finally cried. "*Charge!*" Despite the order, the infantry continued at their same relentless walking pace. They quickly overran One.

"Once again One is ours," said the Colonel. "Forgive me for not clapping."

"I don't think you understand the strategic importance of One," said the General. "Without it, we can never get to Two."

"Yes, it's highly strategic. Didn't we take it twice yesterday, and the day before, and the day before? But it doesn't do anything to protect us from the jets attacking every minute and the tanks attacking every hour."

"That's why it's called war." The army continued its relentless march, with the fighter jets again strafing them.

"Enemy behind!" cried the Colonel a few min-

utes later. "And above!" Sure enough, not only were the fighter jets strafing them from above, but a tank battalion had come charging from behind them, turrets blazing. "Should we hit the dirt?" he asked, but he knew the answer.

"*Onward!*" the General cried, even as a bomb burst a few feet away. "Left flank go left, right flank go right!"

As the army split into two, the tank battalion charged past in the middle, firing at them as they went by. They fired back, but their bullets just bounced off the heavy armor.

"General Longhand always falls for that maneuver," said the General of his counterpart. If only they had RPGs or anti-aircraft guns they could take out more tanks and jets, but the bureaucrats at Twelve always said they had none to spare. He raised his voice. "*Converge forces!*" and the army merged back again. "*Onward!*"

A minute later jets came in for another strafing run.

"Fire at the lead one!" cried the General. As it passed overhead, the entire army blistered it with withering fire. Several puffs of smoke shot out of the jet—and then it exploded in flames. As the army cheered, it dove down and crashed in even more flames and smoke.

But the strafing had once again taken a toll. The dead lay on the ground all about, but the soldiers never slowed their pace.

After the next strafing attack, the Colonel said, "I've been timing these attacks on my watch. The jets seem to pass each of the twelve strategic points every sixty seconds, the tanks every sixty minutes. But since we're marching away from them, the jets attack us about every 61 seconds, the tanks every 65. Maybe we should use that info to prepare for them? Hit the dirt before the jets arrive, and turn and begin firing when the tanks approach?"

"Great idea, Colonel," said the General. "But that'll slow us down. It's all a trick by General Skinnyhand—he's a former ace, you know—and General Longhand, who learned from Patton and Rommel. The moment we start anticipating them, they'll change their timing and sneak up on us. We'll continue marching at all costs."

Many more soldiers were lost in each of the attacks, but they continued to march, and they took over Two, Three, Four, and Five. Soon they were on the verge of taking Six, even as Skinnyhand's fighter jets strafed them.

"Victory is again ours!" cried the General as they overran Six. "We will—"

But he and the infantry flinched at a sudden loud sound coming from seemingly everywhere, like a jackhammer, a blaring that might wake the dead.

"*Make it stop!*" someone cried as they covered their ears. The vibrating ground made the General instantly nauseous.

A gigantic, gnarled fist, with grayish hairs between its knuckles, rose above them and slammed into the top of the world. The ground beneath them shook, knocking many off their feet. The blaring abruptly stopped.

Many soldiers panicked and seemed about to stop. "*Continue forward!*" cried the General. The fist pulled away and disappeared into the beyond. "I hate that thing," he muttered. Then, to his soldiers, he cried, "*Onward!*"

"I've been keeping track of that big, hairy hand," said the Colonel. "It shows up every other time we reach Six. But after appearing five out of ten times, always alternating, it skips the next four times. And then the cycle repeats. Very strange."

"Great work, Colonel. Next time it's about to attack, let me know and we'll throw all our firepower at it." Which would be like throwing pebbles at Godzilla.

"So what now?" asked the Colonel. "I'm getting this déjà vu feeling of déjà vu."

"We will do as we were ordered and march on. Seven is a highly strategic target."

"We've been doing this *forever!*" the Colonel cried. "We take One, we take Two, we take Three, and we keep doing that until we take Twelve, and then we do it all over again, hup, two, three, four! It's like we're going in circles. What is our purpose, General?"

"Our purpose?" The General scowled. "Our purpose is to do what we are ordered to do. We were ordered to move forward, and so we shall move forward until we are ordered to stop. We'll take Seven, Eight, and so on up to Twelve, where we'll get fresh recruits and supplies, and maybe we'll finally get those RPGs and anti-aircraft guns, and then we'll keep on going until ordered to stop. Are we clear, soldier?"

"Yes sir!"

"*Are we clear?*"

"Crystal, sir!"

The General raised Hickory and pointed it forward. "*Onward!*" The army continued its march.

Just then there was another strafing run. A bullet smashed into the Colonel's head, and he wordlessly fell to the ground. The General stared, openmouthed, and came to a stop. His troops followed suit, many gathering about him.

"*You bloody bastards!*" the General roared. With a tremendous heave, he threw Hickory at the passing jets. It shot into the air, higher and higher, and then it fell back to the ground, coming nowhere near the jets. The General silently walked over and picked it up. He shook it at the sky. "If I ever catch you, Skinnyhand, I'm gonna shish kabob you and toss your body at the bureaucrats at Twelve!"

Then he looked at his remaining troops. "The Colonel didn't make it. But I promise you, the rest of you will." Then he cried, "*Onward!*" They continued their march toward Seven.

The General gave one last glance over his shoulder at the crumpled, nearly headless body of the Colonel, to whom he'd made the same promise. Then he shook his head and continued forward, muttering to himself, "There are no promises in war."

The Phantom Tolbukhin

Harry Turtledove

Harry Turtledove is the award-winning author of the alternate history works *The Man with the Iron Heart*, *The Guns of the South*, *How Few Remain* (winner of the Sidewise Award for Best Novel), the *Worldwar* saga, the *Colonization* books, the *Great War* epics, and the *American Empire* novels. Turtledove is married to fellow novelist Laura Frankos. They have three daughters: Alison, Rachel, and Rebecca. "The Phantom Tolbukhin" originally appeared in *Alternate Generals*.

GENERAL FEDOR TOLBUKHIN TURNED to his political commissar. "Is everything in your area of responsibility in readiness for the assault, Nikita Sergeyevich?"

"FEDOR IVANOVICH, IT IS," Nikita Khrushchev replied. "There can be no doubt that the Fourth Ukrainian Front will win another smashing victory against the fascist lice who suck the blood from the motherland."

Tolbukhin's mouth tightened. Khrushchev should have addressed him as *Comrade General*, not by his first name and patronymic. Political commissars had a way of thinking they were as important as real soldiers. But Khrushchev, unlike some—unlike most—political commissars Tolbukhin knew, was not afraid to get gun oil on his hands, or even to take a PPSh41 submachine gun up to the front line and personally pot a few fascists.

"Will you inspect the troops before ordering them to the assault against Zaporozhye?" Khrushchev asked.

"I will, and gladly," Tolbukhin replied.

Not all of Tolbukhin's forces were drawn up for inspection, of course: too great a danger of marauding *Luftwaffe* fighters spotting such an assemblage and shooting it up. But representatives from each of the units the Soviet general had welded into a solid fighting force were there, lined up behind the red banners that symbolized their proud records. Yes, they were all there: the flags of the First Guards Army, the Second Guards, the Eighth Guards, the Fifth Shock Army, the Thirty-Eighth Army, and the Fifty-First.

"Comrade Standard Bearer!" Tolbukhin said to the young soldier who carried the flag of the Eighth Guards Army, which bore the images of Marx and Lenin and Stalin.

"I serve the Soviet Union, Comrade General!" the standard bearer barked. But for his lips, he was utterly motionless. By his wide Slavic face, he might have come from anywhere in the USSR; his mouth proved him a native Ukrainian, for he turned the Great Russian G into an H.

"We all serve the Soviet Union," Tolbukhin said. "How may we best serve the motherland?"

"By expelling from her soil the German invaders," the young soldier replied. "Only then can we take back what is ours. Only then can we begin to build true Communism. It surely will come in my lifetime."

"It surely will," Tolbukhin said. He nodded to Khrushchev, who marched one pace to his left, one pace to the rear. "If all the men are as well indoctrinated as this one, the Fourth Ukrainian Front cannot fail."

After inspecting the detachments, he conferred with the army commanders—and, inevitably, with their political commissars. They crowded a tumbledown barn to overflowing. By the light of a kerosene lantern, Tolbukhin bent over the map, pointing out the avenues of approach the forces would use. Lieutenant General Yuri Kuznetsov, commander of the Eighth Guards Army, grinned wide enough to show a couple of missing teeth. "It is a good plan, Comrade General," he said. "The invaders will regret ever setting foot in the Soviet Union."

"I thank you, Yuri Nikolaievich," Tolbukhin said. "Your knowledge of the approach roads to the city will help the attack succeed."

"The fascist invaders *already* regret ever setting foot in the Soviet Union," Khrushchev said loudly.

Lieutenant General Kuznetsov dipped his head, accepting the rebuke. "I serve the Soviet Union!" he said, as if he were a raw recruit rather than a veteran of years of struggle against the Hitlerites.

"You have the proper Soviet spirit," Tolbukhin said, and even the lantern light was enough to show how Kuznetsov flushed with pleasure.

Lieutenant General Ivanov of the First Guards Army turned to Major General Rudzikovich, who had recently assumed command of the Fifth Shock Army, and murmured, "Sure as the devil's grandmother, the Phantom will make the Nazis pay."

Tolbukhin didn't think he was supposed to hear. But he was young for his rank—only fifty-three—and his ears were keen. The nickname warmed him. He'd earned it earlier in the war— the seemingly endless war—against the madmen and ruffians and murderers who followed the swastika. He'd always had a knack for hitting the enemies of the peasants and workers of the Soviet Union where they least expected it, then fading away before they could strike back at his forces.

"Has anyone any questions about the plan before we continue the war for the liberation of Zaporozhye and all the territory of the Soviet Union now groaning under the oppressor's heel?" he asked.

He thought no one would answer, but Rudzikovich spoke up: "Comrade General, are we truly wise to attack the city from the northeast and southeast at the same time? Would we not be better off concentrating our forces for a single strong blow?"

"This is the plan the council of the Fourth Ukrainian Front has made, and this is the plan we shall follow," Khrushchev said angrily.

"Gently, gently," Tolbukhin told his political commissar. He turned back to Rudzikovich. "When we hit the Germans straight on, that is where we run into trouble. Is it not so, Anatoly Pavlovich? We will surprise them instead, and see how they like that."

"I hope it won't be too expensive, that's all," Major General Rudzikovich said. "We have to watch that we spend our brave Soviet soldiers with care these days."

"I know," Tolbukhin answered. "Sooner or later, though, the Nazis have to run out of men." Soviet strategists had been saying that ever since the Germans, callously disregarding the treaty Ribbentrop had signed with Foreign Commissar Molotov, invaded the USSR. General Tolbukhin pointed to the evidence: "See how many Hungarian and Romanian and Italian soldiers they have here in the Ukraine to pad out their own forces."

"And they cannot even station the Hungarians and Romanians next to one another, lest they fight," Khrushchev added—like any political commissar, if he couldn't score points off Rudzikovich one way, he'd try another. "Thieves fall out. It is only one more proof that the dialectic assures our victory. So long as we labor like Stakhanovites, over and above the norm, that victory will be ours."

"Anatoly Pavlovich, we have been over the plan a great many times," Tolbukhin said, almost pleadingly. "If you seek to alter it now, just before the attack goes in, you will need a better reason than 'I hope.'"

Anatoly Rudzikovich shrugged. "I hope you are right, Comrade General," he said, bearing down heavily on the start of the sentence. He shrugged again. "Well, *nichevo*." *It can't be helped* was a Russian foundation old as time.

Tolbukhin said, "Collect your detachments, Comrades, and rejoin your main forces. The attack will go in on time. And we shall strike the fascists a heavy blow at Zaporozhye. For Stalin and the motherland!"

"For Stalin and the motherland!" his lieutenants chorused. They left the barn with their political commissars—all but Lieutenant General Yuri Kuznetsov, whose Eighth Guards Army was based at Collective Farm 122 nearby.

"This attack *must* succeed, Fedor Ivanovich," Khrushchev said quietly. "The situation in the Ukraine requires it."

"I understand that, Nikita Sergeyevich," Tolbukhin answered, as quietly. "To make sure the attack succeeds, I intend to go in with the leading wave of troops. Will you fight at my side?"

In the dim light, he watched Khrushchev. Most political commissars would have looked for the nearest bed under which to hide at a request like that. Khrushchev only nodded. "Of course I will."

"Stout fellow." Tolbukhin slapped him on the back. He gathered up Kuznetsov and his political commissar by eye. "Let's go."

The night was very black. The moon, nearly new, would not rise till just before sunup. Only starlight shone down on Tolbukhin and his comrades. He nodded to himself. The armies grouped together into the Fourth Ukrainian Front would be all the harder for German planes to spot before they struck Zaporozhye. Dispersing them would help there, too.

He wished for air cover, then shrugged. He'd wished for a great many things in life he'd ended up not receiving. He remained alive to do more wishing. *One day,* he thought, *and one day soon, may we see more airplanes blazoned with the red star.* He was too well indoctrinated a Marxist-Leninist to recognize that as a prayer.

Waiting outside Collective Farm 122 stood the men of the Eighth Guards Army. Lieutenant General Kuznetsov spoke to them: "General Tolbukhin not only sends us into battle against the Hitlerite oppressors and bandits, he leads us into battle against them. Let us cheer the Comrade General!"

"*Urra!*" The cheer burst from the soldiers' throats, but softly, cautiously. Most of the men were veterans of many fights against the Nazis. They knew better than to give themselves away too soon.

However soft those cheers, they heartened Tolbukhin. "We shall win tonight," he said, as if no other alternative were even imaginable. "We shall win for Comrade Stalin, we shall win for the memory of the great Lenin, we shall win for the motherland."

"We serve the Soviet Union!" the soldiers chorused. Beside Tolbukhin, Khrushchev's broad peasant face showed a broad peasant grin. These were indeed well-indoctrinated men.

They were also devilishly good fighters. To Tolbukhin's mind, that counted for more. He spoke one word: "*Vryed'!*" Obedient to his order, the soldiers of the Eighth Guards Army trotted forward.

Tolbukhin trotted along with them. So did Khrushchev. Both the general and the political commissar were older and rounder than the soldiers they commanded. They would not have lost much face had they failed to keep up. Tolbukhin intended to lose no face whatever. His heart pounded. His lungs burned. His legs began to ache. He kept on nonetheless. So did Khrushchev, grimly slogging along beside him.

He expected the first brush with the *Wehrmacht* to take place outside of Zaporozhye, and so it did. The Germans patrolled east of the city: no denying they were technically competent soldiers. Tolbukhin wished they were less able; that would have spared the USSR endless grief.

A voice came out of the night: "*Wer geht hier?*" A hail of rifle and submachine-gun bullets answered that German hail. Tolbukhin hoped his men wiped out the patrol before the Nazis could use their wireless set. When the Germans stopped shooting back, which took only moments, the Eighth Guards Army rolled on.

Less than ten minutes later, planes rolled out of the west. Along with the soldiers in the first ranks, Tolbukhin threw himself flat. He ground his teeth and cursed under his breath. Had that patrol got a signal out after all? He hoped it was not so. Had prayer been part of his ideology, he would have prayed it was not so. If the Germans learned of the assault too soon, they could blunt it with artillery and rockets at minimal cost to themselves.

The planes—Tolbukhin recognized the silhouettes of Focke-Wulf 190s—zoomed away. They dropped neither bombs nor flares, and did not strafe the men of the Fourth Ukrainian Front.

Tolbukhin scrambled to his feet. "Onward!" he called.

Onward the men went. Tolbukhin felt a glow of pride. After so much war, after so much heartbreak, they still retained their revolutionary spirit. "Truly, these are the New Soviet Men," he called to Khrushchev.

A middle-aged Soviet man, the political commissar nodded. "We shall never rest until we drive the last of the German invaders from our soil. As Comrade Stalin said, 'Not one step back!' Once the fascists are gone, we shall rebuild this land to our hearts' desire."

Tolbukhin's heart's desire was piles of dead Germans in field-gray uniforms, clouds of flies swarming over their stinking bodies. And he had achieved his heart's desire many times. But however many Nazis the men under his command killed, more kept coming out of the west. It hardly seemed fair.

Ahead loomed the apartment blocks and factories of Zaporozhye, black against the dark night sky. German patrols enforced their blackout by shooting into lighted windows. If they hit a Russian mother or a sleeping child...it bothered them not in the least. Maybe they won promotion for it.

"Kuznetsov," Tolbukhin called through the night.

"Yes, Comrade General?" the commander of the Eighth Guards Army asked.

"Lead the First and Second Divisions by way of Tregubenko Boulevard," Tolbukhin said. "I will take the Fifth and Ninth Divisions farther south, by way of Metallurgov Street. Thus we will converge upon the objective."

"I serve the Soviet Union!" Kuznetsov said.

Zaporozhye had already been fought over a good many times. As Tolbukhin got into the outskirts of the Ukrainian city, he saw the gaps bombs and shellfire had torn in the buildings. People still lived in those battered blocks of flats and still labored in those factories under German guns.

In the doorway to one of those apartment

blocks, a tall, thin man in the field-gray tunic and trousers of the *Wehrmacht* was kissing and feeling up a blond woman whose overalls said she was a factory worker. *A factory worker supplementing her income as a Nazi whore,* Tolbukhin thought coldly.

At the sound of booted feet running on Metallurgov Street, the German soldier broke away from the Ukrainian woman. He shouted something. Submachine-gun fire from the advancing Soviet troops cut him down. The woman fell, too, fell and fell screaming. Khrushchev stopped beside her and shot her in the back of the neck. The screams cut off.

"Well done, Nikita Sergeyevich," Tolbukhin said.

"I've given plenty of traitors what they deserve," Khrushchev answered. "I know how. And it's always a pleasure."

"Yes," Tolbukhin said: of course a commissar would see a traitor where he saw a whore. "We'll have to move faster now, though; the racket will draw the fascists. *Nichevo.* We'd have bumped into another Nazi patrol in a minute or two, anyway."

One thing the racket did not do was bring people out of their flats to join the Eighth Guards Army in the fight against the fascist occupiers. As the soldiers ran, they shouted, "Citizens of Zaporozhye, the hour of liberation is at hand!" But the city had seen a lot of war. Civilians left here were no doubt cowering under their beds, hoping no stray bullets from either Soviet or German guns would find them.

"Scouts forward!" Tolbukhin shouted as his men turned south from Metallurgov onto Pravdy Street. They were getting close to their objective. The fascists surely had guards in the area—but where? Finding them before they set eyes on the men of the Eighth Guards Army could make the difference between triumph and disaster.

Then the hammering of gunfire broke out to the south. Khrushchev laughed out loud. "The Nazis will think they are engaging the whole of our force, Fedor Ivanovich," he said joyfully. "For

who would think even the Phantom dared divide his men so?"

Tolbukhin ran on behind the scouts. The Nazis were indeed pulling soldiers to the south to fight the fire there, and didn't discover they were between two fires till the Eighth Guards Army and, moments later, the men of the Fifth Shock Army and the Fifty-First Army opened up on them as well. How the Hitlerites howled!

Ahead of him, a German machine gun snarled death—till grenades put the men handling it out of action. Then, a moment later, it started up again, this time with Red Army soldiers feeding it and handling the trigger. Tolbukhin whooped with glee. An MG-42 was a powerful weapon. Turning it on its makers carried the sweetness of poetic justice.

One of his soldiers pointed and shouted: "The objective! The armory! And look, Comrade General! Some of our men are already inside. We have succeeded."

"We have not succeeded yet," Tolbukhin answered. "We will have succeeded only when we have done what he came here to do." He raised his voice to a great shout: "Form a perimeter around the building. Exploitation teams, forward! You know your assignments."

"Remember, soldiers of the Soviet Union, the motherland depends on your courage and discipline," Khrushchev added.

As Tolbukhin had planned, the perimeter force around the Nazi armory was as small as possible; the exploitation force, made up of teams from each army of the Fourth Ukrainian Front, as large. Tolbukhin went into the armory with the exploitation force. Its mission here was far the most important for the strike against Zaporozhye.

Inside the armory, German efficiency came to the aid of the Soviet Union. The Nazis had arranged weapons and ammunition so their own troops could lay hold of whatever they needed as quickly as possible. The men of the Red Army happily seized rifles and submachine guns and the ammunition that went with each. They also laid hands on a couple of more MG-42s. If they could get those out of the city, the fascists would regret it whenever they tried driving down a road for a hundred kilometers around.

"When you're loaded up, get out!" Tolbukhin shouted. "Pretty soon, the Nazis will hit us with everything they've got." He did not disdain slinging a German rifle on his back and loading his pockets with clips of ammunition.

"We have routed them, Fedor Ivanovich," Khrushchev said. When Tolbukhin did not reply, the political commissar added, "A million rubles for your thoughts, Comrade General."

Before the war, the equivalent sum would have been a *kopeck*. Of course, before the war Tolbukhin would not have called the understrength regiment he led a front. Companies would not have been styled armies, nor sections divisions. "Inflation is everywhere," he murmured, and then spoke to Khrushchev: "As long as you came in, Nikita Sergeyevich, load up, and then we'll break away if we can, if the Germans let us."

Khrushchev affected an injured look. "Am I then only a beast of burden, Fedor Ivanovich?"

"We are all only beasts of burden in the building of true Communism," Tolbukhin replied, relishing the chance to get off one of those sententious bromides at the political commissar's expense. He went on, "I am not too proud to load myself like a beast of burden. Why should you be?"

Khrushchev flushed and glared furiously. In earlier days—in happier days, though Tolbukhin would not have thought so at the time—upbraiding a political commissar would surely have caused a denunciation to go winging its way up through the Party hierarchy, perhaps all the way up to Stalin himself. So many good men had disappeared in the purges that turned the USSR upside down and inside out between 1936 and 1938: Tukhashevsky and Koniev, Yegorov and Blyukher, Zhukov and Uborevich, Gamarnik and Fedko. Was it any wonder the Red Army had fallen to pieces when the Nazis attacked in May 1941?

And now, in 1947, Khrushchev was as high-ranking a political commissar as remained among the living. To whom could he denounce Tolbukhin? No one, and he knew it. However furious he was, he started filling his pockets with magazines of Mauser and Schmeisser rounds.

Sometimes, Tolbukhin wondered why he persisted in the fight against the fascists when the system he served, even in its tattered remnants, was so onerous. The answer was not hard to find. For one thing, he understood the difference between bad and worse. And, for another, he'd been of general's rank when the Hitlerites invaded the motherland. If they caught him, they would liquidate him—their methods in the Soviet Union made even Stalin's seem mild by comparison. If he kept fighting, he might possibly—just possibly—succeed.

Khrushchev clanked when turning back to him. The tubby little political commissar was still glaring. "I am ready, Fedor Ivanovich," he said. "I hope you are satisfied."

"*Da*," Tolbukhin said. He hadn't been satisfied since Moscow and Leningrad fell, but Khrushchev couldn't do anything about that. Tolbukhin pulled from his pocket an officer's whistle and blew a long, furious blast. "Soldiers of the Red Army, we have achieved our objective!" he shouted in a great voice. "Now we complete the mission by making our departure!"

He was none too soon. Outside, the fascists were striking heavy blows against his perimeter teams. But the fresh men coming out of the armory gave the Soviets new strength and let them blast open a corridor to the east and escape.

Now it was every section—every division, in the grandiose language of what passed for the Red Army in the southern Ukraine these days—for itself. Inevitably, men fell as the units made their way out of Zaporozhye and onto the steppe. Tolbukhin's heart sobbed within him each time he saw a Soviet soldier go down. Recruits were so hard to come by these days. The booty he'd gained from this raid would help there, and would also help bring some of the bandit bands prowling the steppe under the operational control of the Red Army. With more men, with more guns, he'd be able to hurt the Nazis more the next time.

But if, before he got out of Zaporozhye, he lost all the men he had now... *What then, Comrade General?* he jeered at himself.

Bullets cracked around him, spattering off concrete and striking blue sparks when they ricocheted from metal. He lacked the time to be afraid. He had to keep moving, keep shouting orders, keep turning back and sending another burst of submachine-gun fire at the pursuing Hitlerites.

Then his booted feet thudded on dirt, not on asphalt or concrete any more. "Out of the city!" he cried exultantly.

And there, not far away, Khrushchev doggedly pounded along. He had grit, did the political commissar. "Scatter!" he called to the men within the sound of his voice. "Scatter and hide your booty in the secure places. Resume the *maskirovka* that keeps us all alive."

Without camouflage, the Red Army would long since have become extinct in this part of the USSR. As things were, Tolbukhin's raiders swam like fish through the water of the Soviet peasantry, as Mao's Red Chinese did in their long guerrilla struggle against the imperialists of Japan.

But Tolbukhin had little time to think about Mao, either, for the Germans were going fishing. Nazis on foot, Nazis in armored cars and personnel carriers, and even a couple of panzers came forth from Zaporozhye. At night, Tolbukhin feared the German foot soldiers more than the men in machines. Machines were easy to elude in the darkness. The infantry would be the ones who knew what they were doing.

Still, this was not the first raid Tolbukhin had led against the Germans, nor the tenth, nor the fiftieth, either. What he did not know about rear guards and ambushes wasn't worth knowing. His men stung the Germans again and again, stung them and then crept away. They understood the art of making many men seem few, few seem many. Little by little, they shook off pursuit.

Tolbukhin scrambled down into a *balka* with Khrushchev and half a dozen men from the Eighth Guards Army, then struggled up the other side of the dry wash. They started back toward Collective Farm 122, where, when they were not raiding, they labored for their Nazi masters as they had formerly labored for their Soviet masters.

"Wait," Tolbukhin called to them, his voice low but urgent. "I think we still have Germans on our tail. This is the best place I can think of to make them regret it."

"We serve the Soviet Union!" one of the soldiers said. They returned and took cover behind bushes and stones. So did Tolbukhin. He could not have told anyone how or why he believed the fascists remained in pursuit of this little band, but he did. *Instinct of the hunted,* he thought.

And the instinct did not fail him. Inside a quarter of an hour, men in coal-scuttle helmets began going down into the *balka*. One of them tripped, stumbled, and fell with a thud. "Those God-damned stinking Russian pigdogs," he growled in guttural German. "They'll pay for this. Screw me out of sack time, will they?"

"*Ja,* better we should screw their women than they should screw us out of sack time," another trooper said. "That Natasha in the soldiers' brothel, she's limber like she doesn't have any bones at all."

"Heinrich, Klaus, *shut up!*" another voice hissed. "You've got to play the game like those Red bastards are waiting for us on the far side of this miserable gully. You don't, your family gets a *Fallen for Führer and Fatherland* telegram one fine day." By the way the other two men fell silent, Tolbukhin concluded that fellow was a corporal or sergeant. From his hiding place, he kept an eye on the sensible Nazi. *I'll shoot you first,* he thought.

Grunting and cursing—but cursing in whispers now—the Germans started making their way up the side of the *balka*. Yes, there was the one who kept his mind on business. Kill enough of that kind and the rest grew less efficient. The Germans got rid of Soviet officers and commissars on the same brutal logic.

Closer, closer…A submachine gun spat a great number of bullets, but was hardly a weapon of finesse or accuracy. "Fire!" Tolbukhin shouted, and blazed away. The Nazi noncom tumbled down the steep side of the wash. Some of those bullets had surely bitten him. The rest of the German squad lasted only moments longer. One of the Hitlerites lay groaning till a Red Army man went down and cut his throat. Who could guess how long he might last otherwise? Too long, maybe.

"*Now* we go on home," Tolbukhin said.

They had practiced withdrawal from such raids many times before, and *maskirovka* came naturally to Soviet soldiers. They took an indirect route back to the collective farm, concealing their tracks as best they could. The Hitlerites sometimes hunted them with dogs. They knew how to deal with that, too. Whenever they came to rivulets running through the steppe, they trampled along in them for a couple of hundred meters, now going one way, now the other. A couple of them also had their canteens filled with fiery pepper-flavored vodka. They poured some on their trail every now and then; it drove the hounds frantic.

"Waste of good vodka," one of the soldiers grumbled.

"If it keeps us alive, it isn't wasted," Tolbukhin said. "If it keeps us alive, we can always get outside of more later."

"The Comrade General is right," Khrushchev said. Where he was often too familiar with Tolbukhin, he was too formal with the men.

This time, though, it turned out not to matter. One of the other soldiers gave the fellow who'd complained a shot in the ribs with his elbow. "*Da*, Volya, the Phantom is right," he said. "The Phantom's been right a lot of times, and he hasn't hardly been wrong yet. Let's give a cheer for the Phantom."

It was another soft cheer, because they weren't quite safe yet, but a cheer nonetheless: "*Urra* for the Phantom Tolbukhin!"

Maybe, Tolbukhin thought as a grin stretched itself across his face, *maybe we'll lick the Hitlerites yet, in spite of everything.* He didn't know whether he believed that or not. He knew he'd keep trying. He trotted on. Collective Farm 122 wasn't far now.

The Battle of Dorking

GEORGE TOMKYNS CHESNEY

George Tomkyns Chesney (1830–1895) rose to the rank of general in the British army in 1892, but wrote "The Battle of Dorking" as a lieutenant colonel just after the 1870–1871 Franco-Prussian War. This story is one of the first—if not *the* first—piece of speculative military fiction on record, an alternate history tale positing a Prussian invasion of England after victory over France. This story cautions against a lack of national preparedness at a time when land warfare was transitioning from single-shot small arms and massed infantry to industrialized warfare with railroads, rifled artillery, rapid-fire small arms, and infantry in open order. "The Battle of Dorking" was originally published in *Blackwood's Magazine* in 1871, to widespread acclaim, sparking intense interest in this new form of literature. This story has been edited to modernize punctuation and add paragraphing, while maintaining modern British spelling.

YOU ASK ME TO tell you, my grandchildren, something about my own share in the great events that happened fifty years ago. 'Tis sad work turning back to that bitter page in our history, but you may perhaps take profit in your new homes from the lesson it teaches.

FOR US IN ENGLAND it came too late. And yet we had plenty of warnings, if we had only made use of them. The danger did not come on us unawares.

It burst on us suddenly, 'tis true; but its coming was foreshadowed plainly enough to open our eyes, if we had not been wilfully blind. We English have only ourselves to blame for the humiliation which has been brought on the land. Venerable old age! Dishonourable old age, I say, when it follows a manhood dishonoured as ours has been. I declare, even now, though fifty years have passed, I can hardly look a young man in the face when I think I am one of those in whose youth happened this degradation of Old England—one of those who betrayed the trust handed down to us unstained by our forefathers.

What a proud and happy country was this fifty years ago![1] Free trade had been working for more than a quarter of a century, and there seemed to be no end to the riches it was bringing us. London was growing bigger and bigger; you could not build houses fast enough for the rich people who wanted to live in them, the merchants who made the money and came from all parts of the world to settle there, and the lawyers and doctors and engineers and others, and tradespeople who got their share out of the profits. The streets reached down to Croydon and Wimbledon, which my father could remember quite country places; and people used to say that Kingston and Reigate would soon be joined to London.

We thought we could go on building and multiplying for ever. 'Tis true that even then there was no lack of poverty; the people who had no money went on increasing as fast as the rich, and pauperism was already beginning to be a difficulty; but if the rates were high, there was plenty of money to pay them with; and as for what were called the middle classes, there really seemed no limit to their increase and prosperity. People in those days thought it quite a matter of course to bring a dozen children into the world—or, as it used to be said, Providence sent them that number of babies; and if they couldn't always marry off all the daughters, they used to manage to provide for the sons, for there were new openings

to be found in all the professions, or in the government offices, which went on steadily getting larger. Besides, in those days young men could be sent out to India, or into the army or navy; and even then emigration was not uncommon, although not the regular custom it is now. Schoolmasters, like all other professional classes, drove a capital trade. They did not teach very much, to be sure, but new schools with their four or five hundred boys were springing up all over the country.

Fools that we were! We thought that all this wealth and prosperity were sent us by Providence, and could not stop coming. In our blindness we did not see that we were merely a big workshop, making up the things which came from all parts of the world; and that if other nations stopped sending us raw goods to work up, we could not produce them ourselves. True, we had in those days an advantage in our cheap coal and iron; and had we taken care not to waste the fuel, it might have lasted us longer.

But even then there were signs that coal and iron would soon become cheaper in foreign parts; while as to food and other things, England was not better off than it is now. We were so rich simply because other nations from all parts of the world were in the habit of sending their goods to us to be sold or manufactured; and we thought that this would last for ever. And so, perhaps, it might have lasted, if we had only taken proper means to keep it; but, in our folly, we were too careless even to insure our prosperity, and after the course of trade was turned away it would not come back again.

---

[1]Chesney set his story in 1921 then reflected on the fifty years since the Prussian invasion, which is a fascinating commentary on the difference between prediction and forecasting. Chesney could not have known about technologies such as aircraft, tanks, high explosives, radio communications, or long-range artillery (and what effect these would have on warfare), but he was clearly aware of railroads, mass conscription systems, and rifled weapons. When it came to preparing for war, his extrapolation was no less insightful for being wrong.

AND YET, IF EVER a nation had a plain warning, we had. If we were the greatest trading country, our neighbours were the leading military power in Europe.[2] They were driving a good trade, too, for this was before their foolish communism (about which you will hear when you are older) had ruined the rich without benefiting the poor, and they were in many respects the first nation in Europe; but it was on their army that they prided themselves most. And with reason. They had beaten the Russians and the Austrians, and the Prussians too, in bygone years, and they thought they were invincible.

Well do I remember the great review held at Paris by the Emperor Napoleon during the great Exhibition, and how proud he looked showing off his splendid Guards to the assembled kings and princes.[3] Yet, three years afterwards, the force so long deemed the first in Europe was ignominiously beaten, and the whole army taken prisoners. Such a defeat had never happened before in the world's history; and with this proof before us of the folly of disbelieving in the possibility of disaster merely because it had never fallen upon us, it might have been supposed that we should have the sense to take the lesson to heart.

And the country was certainly roused for a time, and a cry was raised that the army ought to be reorganized, and our defences strengthened against the enormous power for sudden attacks which it was seen other nations were able to put forth. And a scheme of army reform was brought forward by the government. It was a half-and-half affair at best; and unfortunately, instead of being taken up in Parliament as a national scheme, it was made a party matter of, and so fell through.

There was a Radical section of the House, too, whose votes had to be secured by conciliation, and which blindly demanded a reduction of armaments as the price of allegiance. This party always decried military establishments as part of a fixed policy for reducing the influence of the Crown and the aristocracy. They could not understand that the times had altogether changed, that the Crown had really no power, and that the government merely existed at the pleasure of the House of Commons, and that even Parliament-rule was beginning to give way to mob law.

At any rate, the Ministry, baffled on all sides, gave up by degrees all the strong points of a scheme which they were not heartily in earnest about. It was not that there was any lack of money, if only it had been spent in the right way. The army cost enough, and more than enough, to give us a proper defence, and there were armed men of sorts in plenty and to spare, if only they had been decently organized. It was in organization and forethought that we fell short, because our rulers did not heartily believe in the need for preparation. The fleet and the Channel, they said, were sufficient protection.

So army reform was put off to some more convenient season, and the militia and volunteers were left untrained as before, because to call them out for drill would "interfere with the industry of the country." We could have given up some of the industry of those days, forsooth, and yet be busier than we are now. But why tell you a tale you have so often heard already? The nation,

---

[2] Before the Franco-Prussian War (1870–1871), observers regarded France as the unquestioned land power on the continent. Armed forces around the world emulated French patterns of military practice, but this all came crashing down in August and September of 1870. In *Road to Sedan*, historian Edward Richard Holmes quoted one post-war commentator, describing French officers as "brave to excess, confident in their luck, loved by their men because they were concerned with them and were regularly seen by them: these leaders had coup d'oeil, decision, in a word all the qualities acquired by experience, but they did not understand war." Chesney was certainly aware of assessments like this.

[3] Most observers (with notable exceptions, such as the French military attaché in Berlin) expected a quick French victory against the Prussian army. France was led by the nephew of Napoleon, Charles Louis Napoléon Bonaparte (Napoleon III) and its forces were unstoppable in its colonial wars. Stark realization fell at the decisive Battle of Sedan (1–2 September 1870), where Prussian forces surrounded and annihilated France's entire second-line army (the first-line army was then besieged at Metz), capturing over 500 guns and 100,000 men, including Emperor Napoleon III himself. Chesney's readers at the time would certainly have been aware of these events.

although uneasy, was misled by the false security its leaders professed to feel; and the warning given by the disasters that overtook France was allowed to pass by unheeded. We would not even be at the trouble of putting our arsenals in a safe place, or of guarding the capital against a surprise, although the cost of doing so would not have been so much as missed from the national wealth. The French trusted in their army and its great reputation, we in our fleet; and in each case the result of this blind confidence was disaster, such as our forefathers in their hardest struggles could not have even imagined.

I NEED HARDLY TELL YOU how the crash came about. First, the rising in India drew away a part of our small army[4]; then came the difficulty with America, which had been threatening for years, and we sent off ten thousand men to defend Canada—a handful which did not go far to strengthen the real defences of that country, but formed an irresistible temptation to the Americans to try and take them prisoners, especially as the contingent included three battalions of the Guards. Thus the regular army at home was even smaller than usual, and nearly half of it was in Ireland to check the talked-of Fenian invasion fitting out in the West.[5]

Worse still—though I do not know it would really have mattered as things turned out—the fleet was scattered abroad: some ships to guard the West Indies, others to check privateering in the China seas, and a large part to try and protect our colonies on the Northern Pacific shore of America, where, with incredible folly, we continued to retain possessions which we could not possibly defend. America was not the great power forty years ago that it is now; but for us to try and hold territory on her shores which could only be reached by sailing round the Horn, was as absurd as if she had attempted to take the Isle of Man before the independence of Ireland. We see this plainly enough now, but we were all blind then.

It was while we were in this state, with our ships all over the world, and our little bit of an army cut up into detachments, that the Secret Treaty was published, and Holland and Denmark were annexed. People say now that we might have escaped the troubles which came on us if we had at any rate kept quiet till our other difficulties were settled; but the English were always an impulsive lot: the whole country was boiling over with indignation, and the government, egged on by the press, and going with the stream, declared war. We had always got out of scrapes before, and we believed our old luck and pluck would somehow pull us through.

Then, of course, there was bustle and hurry all over the land. Not that the calling up of the army reserves caused much stir, for I think there were only about 5,000 altogether, and a good many of these were not to be found when the time came; but recruiting was going on all over the country,

---

[4]Throughout the late 1700s and early 1800s, the British East India Company (operating on behalf of the Crown) consolidated effective control over India through a mix of clever diplomacy, efficient administration, and the timely application of military violence. The Company maintained an army of about 300,000 Indians and 50,000 British soldiers. In 1857 a significant portion of the Indian soldiers revolted against British rule, and Chesney fought and was wounded in this conflict. The proportion of British soldiers (especially officers) in the British India army increased dramatically after this rising, an episode with which Chesney was intimately familiar, as he served in India from 1881 to 1892.

[5]After the American Civil War, Irish separatists known as Fenians recruited soldiers to fight for Irish independence. Ostensibly, 50,000 men were willing to fight. A Fenian uprising in 1867 was an utter military failure, due to British authorities having thoroughly infiltrated rebel networks. The threat of such uprisings did not dissipate afterwards, however, as evidenced by a Fenian bombing campaign (1881–1885), the Easter Rising (1916), and the War of Independence (1919–1922).

[6]Great Britain boasts a long history of volunteer military recruitment. Even during World War I, there was little serious discussion of conscription until 1917, three years after the outbreak of hostilities. Chesney's readers in 1871 would have understood that 50,000 men being "voted for the army" referred to increasing the incentives to attract volunteer recruits. See Victor Asal, Justin Conrad, and Nathan W. Toronto, "I Want You! The Determinants of Military Conscription," *Journal of Conflict Resolution* 61, no. 7 (2017): 1456–1481.

with a tremendous high bounty, 50,000 more men having been voted for the army.[6] Then there was a Ballot Bill passed for adding 55,500 men to the militia; why a round number was not fixed on I don't know, but the Prime Minister said that this was the exact quota wanted to put the defences of the country on a sound footing. Then the ship-building that began! Ironclads, despatch-boats, gunboats, monitors—every building-yard in the country got its job, and they were offering ten shillings a day wages for anybody who could drive a rivet.

This didn't improve the recruiting, you may suppose.[7] I remember, too, there was a squabble in the House of Commons about whether artisans should be drawn for the ballot, as they were so much wanted, and I think they got an exemption. This sent numbers to the yards; and if we had had a couple of years to prepare instead of a couple of weeks, I daresay we should have done very well.

I T WAS ON A Monday that the declaration of war was announced, and in a few hours we got our first inkling of the sort of preparation the enemy had made for the event which they had really brought about, although the actual declaration was made by us. A pious appeal to the God of battles, whom it was said we had aroused, was telegraphed back; and from that moment all communication with the north of Europe was cut off. Our embassies and legations were packed off at an hour's notice, and it was as if we had suddenly come back to the Middle Ages.

The dumb astonishment visible all over London the next morning, when the papers came out void of news, merely hinting at what had happened, was one of the most startling things in this war of surprises. But everything had been arranged beforehand; nor ought we to have been surprised, for we had seen the same Power, only a few months before, move down half a million of men on a few days' notice, to conquer the greatest military nation in Europe, with no more fuss than our War Office used to make over the transport of a brigade from Aldershot to Brighton—and this, too, without the allies it had now.[8] What happened now was not a bit more wonderful in reality; but people of this country could not bring themselves to believe that what had never occurred before to England could ever possibly happen. Like our neighbours, we became wise when it was too late.

Of course the papers were not long in getting news—even the mighty organization set at work could not shut out a special correspondent; and in a very few days, although the telegraphs and railways were intercepted right across Europe, the main facts oozed out. An embargo had been laid on all the shipping in every port from the Baltic to Ostend; the fleets of the two great Powers had moved out, and it was supposed were assembled in the great northern harbour, and troops were hurrying on board all the steamers detained in these places, most of which were British vessels. It was clear that invasion was intended.

Even then we might have been saved, if the fleet had been ready. The forts which guarded

---

[7] Any form of military recruitment involves strategic tradeoffs, and in the case of Great Britain volunteer recruitment meant an increase in the price of labor. Chesney later makes an oblique reference to military recruitment and training in the Franco-Prussian War. For more on the tradeoff between markets and manpower, see Lindsay P. Cohn and Nathan W. Toronto, "Markets and Manpower: The Political Economy of Compulsory Military Service," *Armed Forces & Society* 43, no. 3 (2017): 436–458.

[8] Military training (and, by extension, mobilization timetables) were pivotal in the Franco-Prussian War. France mobilized its forces before Prussia, yet Prussia had instituted a system of reservist training and mobilization that put many more trained reservists in the field than the French in the first days of the war. Historian William Fortescue, in *The Third Republic in France, 1870–1940*, notes, "The French had not mastered the military use of railways and their mobilization was a shambles; the standard of education and training of most officers and men was well below that of their German counterparts; the German artillery and supply services were better than those of the French; and, unlike the Prussians, the French had no general staff to keep commanders in the field supplied with a regular flow of information and advice. The failure at Sedan was not that of an army, but of a whole system."

the flotilla were perhaps too strong for shipping to attempt; but an ironclad or two, handled as British sailors knew how to use them, might have destroyed or damaged a part of the transports, and delayed the expedition, giving us what we wanted: time.

But then the best part of the fleet had been decoyed down to the Dardanelles, and what remained of the Channel squadron was looking after Fenian filibusters off the west of Ireland; so it was ten days before the fleet was got together, and by that time it was plain the enemy's preparations were too far advanced to be stopped by a coup-de-main. Information, which came chiefly through Italy, came slowly, and was more or less vague and uncertain; but this much was known, that at least a couple of hundred thousand men were embarked or ready to be put on board ships, and that the flotilla was guarded by more ironclads than we could then muster.

I suppose it was the uncertainty as to the point the enemy would aim at for landing, and the fear lest he should give us the go-by, that kept the fleet for several days in the Downs; but it was not until the Tuesday fortnight after the declaration of war that it weighed anchor and steamed away for the North Sea.[9] Of course you have read about the Queen's visit to the fleet the day before, and how she sailed round the ships in her yacht, and went on board the flag-ship to take leave of the admiral; how, overcome with emotion, she told him that the safety of the country was committed to his keeping. You remember, too, the gallant old officer's reply, and how all the ships' yards were manned, and how lustily the tars cheered as her Majesty was rowed off.

The account was of course telegraphed to London, and the high spirits of the fleet infected the whole town. I was outside the Charing Cross station when the Queen's special train from Dover arrived, and from the cheering and shouting which greeted her Majesty as she drove away, you might have supposed we had already won a great victory. The leading journal, which had gone in strongly for the army reduction carried out during the session, and had been nervous and desponding in tone during the past fortnight, suggesting all sorts of compromises as a way of getting out of the war, came out in a very jubilant form next morning. "Panic-stricken inquirers," it said, "ask now, where are the means of meeting the invasion? We reply that the invasion will never take place. A British fleet manned by British sailors, whose courage and enthusiasm are reflected in the people of this country, is already on the way to meet the presumptuous foe. The issue of a contest between British ships and those of any other country, under anything like equal odds, can never be doubtful. England awaits with calm confidence the issue of the impending action."

Such were the words of the leading article, and so we all felt. It was on Tuesday, the 10th of August, that the fleet sailed from the Downs. It took with it a submarine cable to lay down as it advanced, so that continuous communication was kept up, and the papers were publishing special editions every few minutes with the latest news. This was the first time such a thing had been done and the feat was accepted as a good omen. Whether it is true that the Admiralty made use of the cable to keep on sending contradictory orders, which took the command out of the admiral's hands, I can't say; but all that the admiral sent in return was a few messages of the briefest kind, which neither the Admiralty nor any one else could have made any use of. Such a ship had gone off reconnoitring; such another had rejoined—fleet was in latitude so and so.

This went on till the Thursday morning. I had just come up to town by train as usual, and was walking to my office, when the newsboys began to cry, "New edition—enemy's fleet in sight!" You may imagine the scene in London! Business

---

[9]The Downs, near the northeast entrance to the English Channel—off the eastern shore of Kent—offers a sheltered harbor from which ships can patrol the North Sea or the Channel.

still went on at the banks, for bills matured although the independence of the country was being fought out under our own eyes, so to say, and the speculators were active enough. But even with the people who were making and losing their fortunes, the interest in the fleet overcame everything else; men who went to pay in or draw out their money stopped to show the last bulletin to the cashier.

As for the street, you could hardly get along for the crowd stopping to buy and read the papers; while at every house or office the members sat restlessly in the common room, as if to keep together for company, sending out some one of their number every few minutes to get the latest edition. At least this is what happened at our office; but to sit still was as impossible as to do anything, and most of us went out and wandered about among the crowd, under a sort of feeling that the news was got quicker at in this way.

Bad as were the times coming, I think the sickening suspense of that day, and the shock which followed, was almost the worst that we underwent. It was about ten o'clock that the first telegram came; an hour later the wire announced that the admiral had signalled to form line of battle, and shortly afterwards that the order was given to bear down on the enemy and engage. At twelve came the announcement, "Fleet opened fire about three miles to leeward of us"—that is, the ship with the cable. So far all had been expectancy, then came the first token of calamity. "An ironclad has been blown up"—"the enemy's torpedoes are doing great damage"—"the flagship is laid aboard the enemy"—"the flagship appears to be sinking"—"the vice-admiral has signalled to"—there the cable became silent, and, as you know, we heard no more till, two days afterwards, the solitary ironclad which escaped the disaster steamed into Portsmouth.

THEN THE WHOLE STORY came out—how our sailors, gallant as ever, had tried to close with the enemy; how the latter evaded the conflict at close quarters, and, sheering off, left behind them the fatal engines which sent our ships, one after the other, to the bottom; how all this happened almost in a few minutes.[10] The government, it appears, had received warnings of this invention; but to the nation this stunning blow was utterly unexpected.

That Thursday I had to go home early for regimental drill, but it was impossible to remain doing nothing, so when that was over I went up to town again, and after waiting in expectation of news which never came, and missing the midnight train, I walked home. It was a hot, sultry night, and I did not arrive till near sunrise.

The whole town was quite still—the lull before the storm; and as I let myself in with my latchkey, and went softly upstairs to my room to avoid waking the sleeping household, I could not but contrast the peacefulness of the morning— no sound breaking the silence but the singing of the birds in the garden—with the passionate remorse and indignation that would break out with the day. Perhaps the inmates of the rooms were as wakeful as myself, but the house in its stillness was just as it used to be when I came home alone from balls or parties in the happy days gone by. Tired though I was, I could not sleep, so I went down to the river and had a swim; and on returning found the household was assembling for early breakfast.

A sorrowful household it was, although the burden pressing on each was partly an unseen one. My father, doubting whether his firm could last through the day; my mother, her distress about my brother, now with his regiment on the

---

[10]During the American Civil War, with which Chesney and many readers were certainly familiar, rebel Confederate sea mines, especially the Singer Mine, sank 27 U.S. Navy (Union) vessels. Rebel Confederates often used a tactic similar to what Chesney describes here, laying mines so vessels in pursuit sustain damage.

coast, already exceeding that which she felt for the public misfortune, had come down, although hardly fit to leave her room. My sister Clara was worst of all, for she could not but try to disguise her special interest in the fleet; and though we had all guessed that her heart was given to the young lieutenant in the flagship—the first vessel to go down—a love unclaimed could not be told, nor could we express the sympathy we felt for the poor girl. That breakfast, the last meal we ever had together, was soon ended, and my father and I went up to town by an early train, and got there just as the fatal announcement of the loss of the fleet was telegraphed from Portsmouth.

The panic and excitement of that day—how the funds went down to 35; the run upon the bank and its stoppage; the fall of half the houses in the city; how the government issued a notification suspending specie payment and the tendering of bills—this last precaution too late for most firms, Graham & Co. among the number, which stopped payment as soon as my father got to the office; the call to arms and the unanimous response of the country—all this is history which I need not repeat.

You wish to hear about my own share in the business of the time. Well, volunteering had increased immensely from the day war was proclaimed, and our regiment went up in a day or two from its usual strength of 600 to nearly 1,000. But the stock of rifles was deficient. We were promised a further supply in a few days, which however, we never received; and while waiting for them the regiment had to be divided into two parts, the recruits drilling with the rifles in the morning, and we old hands in the evening. The failures and stoppage of work on this black Friday threw an immense number of young men out of employment, and we recruited up to 1,400 strong by the next day; but what was the use of all these men without arms?

On the Saturday it was announced that a lot of smooth-bore muskets in store at the Tower would be served out to regiments applying for them, and a regular scramble took place among the volunteers for them, and our people got hold of a couple of hundred. But you might almost as well have tried to learn rifle-drill with a broomstick as with old brown bess; besides, there was no smooth-bore ammunition in the country. A national subscription was opened for the manufacture of rifles at Birmingham, which ran up to a couple of millions in two days, but, like everything else, this came too late.

To return to the volunteers: camps had been formed a fortnight before at Dover, Brighton, Harwich, and other places, of regulars and militia, and the headquarters of most of the volunteer regiments were attached to one or other of them, and the volunteers themselves used to go down for drill from day to day, as they could spare time, and on Friday an order went out that they should be permanently embodied; but the metropolitan volunteers were still kept about London as a sort of reserve, till it could be seen at what point the invasion would take place.

We were all told off to brigades and divisions. Our brigade consisted of the 4th Royal Surrey Militia, the 1st Surrey Administrative Battalion, as it was called, at Clapham, the 7th Surrey Volunteers at Southwark, and ourselves[11]; but only our battalion and the militia were quartered in the same place, and the whole brigade had merely two or three afternoons together at brigade exercise in Bushey Park before the march took place. Our brigadier belonged to a line regiment in Ireland, and did not join till the very morning the order came.

Meanwhile, during the preliminary fortnight, the militia colonel commanded. But though we volunteers were busy with our drill and preparations, those of us who, like myself, belonged to government offices, had more than enough of office work to do, as you may suppose. The

---

[11]Until World War I, British Army units bore territorial affiliations that were true in both name and practice. Units were raised, bivouacked, and trained locally. After entire towns lost their young men when "Pals Battalions" were destroyed in the trenches, the British Army decided to keep territorial designations but man units from across the country.

volunteer clerks were allowed to leave office at four o'clock, but the rest were kept hard at the desk far into the night. Orders to the lord-lieutenants, to the magistrates, notifications, all the arrangements for cleaning out the work-houses for hospitals—these and a hundred other things had to be managed in our office, and there was as much bustle indoors as out. Fortunate we were to be so busy—the people to be pitied were those who had nothing to do.

And on Sunday (that was the 15th August) work went on just as usual. We had an early parade and drill, and I went up to town by the nine o'clock train in my uniform, taking my rifle with me in case of accidents, and luckily too, as it turned out, a mackintosh overcoat. When I got to Waterloo there were all sorts of rumours afloat. A fleet had been seen off the Downs, and some of the despatch boats which were hovering about the coasts brought news that there was a large flotilla off Harwich, but nothing could be seen from the shore, as the weather was hazy.[12]

The enemy's light ships had taken and sunk all the fishing boats they could catch, to prevent the news of their whereabouts reaching us; but a few escaped during the night and reported that the *Inconstant* frigate coming home from North America without any knowledge of what had taken place, had sailed right into the enemy's fleet and been captured.[13] In town the troops were all getting ready for a move; the Guards in the Wellington Barracks were under arms, and their baggage waggons packed and drawn up in the Birdcage Walk. The usual guard at the Horse Guards had been withdrawn, and orderlies and staff-officers were going to and fro.

All this I saw on the way to my office, where I worked away till twelve o'clock, and then feeling hungry after my early breakfast, I went across Parliament Street to my club to get some luncheon. There were about half-a-dozen men in the coffee-room, none of whom I knew; but in a minute or two Danvers of the Treasury entered in a tremendous hurry. From him I got the first bit of authentic news I had had that day. The enemy had landed in force near Harwich, and the metropolitan regiments were ordered down there to reinforce the troops already collected in that neighbourhood; his regiment was to parade at one o'clock, and he had come to get something to eat before starting. We bolted a hurried lunch, and were just leaving the club when a messenger from the Treasury came running into the hall.

"Oh, Mr. Danvers," said he, "I've come to look for you, sir; the secretary says that all the gentlemen are wanted at the office, and that you must please not one of you go with the regiments."

"The devil!" cried Danvers.

"Do you know if that order extends to all the public offices?" I asked.

"I don't know," said the man, "but I believe it do. I know there's messengers gone round to all the clubs and luncheon-bars to look for the gentlemen; the secretary says it's quite impossible any one can be spared just now, there's so much work to do; there's orders just come to send off our records to Birmingham tonight."

I did not wait to condole with Danvers, but, just glancing up Whitehall to see if any of our messengers were in pursuit, I ran off as hard as I could for Westminster Bridge, and so to the Waterloo station.

<hr>

THE PLACE HAD QUITE changed its aspect since the morning. The regular service of trains had ceased, and the station and approaches were full of troops, among them the Guards and artillery. Everything was very orderly; the men had piled arms, and were standing about in groups. There was no sign of high spirits or enthusiasm. Matters had become too serious.

---

[12] Harwich is about 75 miles east-northeast of London.

[13] According to Admiral George Ballard, writing in 1934, HMS *Inconstant* was an iron-hulled, screw-driven vessel that was the fastest in the world when she was commissioned in 1869. See George A. Ballard, "British Frigates of 1875: The *Inconstant* and *Raleigh*," *Mariner's Mirror* 22, no. 1 (January 1934): 42–53.

Every man's face reflected the general feeling that we had neglected the warnings given us, and that now the danger so long derided as impossible and absurd had really come and found us unprepared. But the soldiers, if grave, looked determined, like men who meant to do their duty whatever might happen.

A train full of guardsmen was just starting for Guildford. I was told it would stop at Surbiton, and, with several other volunteers, hurrying like myself to join our regiment, got a place in it. We did not arrive a moment too soon, for the regiment was marching from Kingston down to the station. The destination of our brigade was the east coast. Empty carriages were drawn up in the siding, and our regiment was to go first. A large crowd was assembled to see it off, including the recruits who had joined during the last fortnight, and who formed by far the largest part of our strength. They were to stay behind, and were certainly very much in the way already; for as all the officers and sergeants belonged to the active part, there was no one to keep discipline among them, and they came crowding around us, breaking the ranks and making it difficult to get into the train.

Here I saw our new brigadier for the first time. He was a soldier-like man, and no doubt knew his duty, but he appeared new to volunteers, and did not seem to know how to deal with gentlemen privates. I wanted very much to run home and get my greatcoat and knapsack, which I had bought a few days ago, but feared to be left behind; a good-natured recruit volunteered to fetch them for me, but he had not returned before we started, and I began the campaign with a kit consisting of a mackintosh and a small pouch of tobacco.

It was a tremendous squeeze in the train for, besides the ten men sitting down, there were three or four standing up in every compartment, and the afternoon was close and sultry, and there were so many stoppages on the way that we took nearly an hour and a half crawling up to Waterloo.

It was between five and six in the afternoon when we arrived there, and it was nearly seven before we marched up to the Shoreditch station. The whole place was filled up with stores and ammunition, to be sent off to the east, so we piled arms in the street and scattered about to get food and drink, of which most of us stood in need, especially the latter, for some were already feeling the worse for the heat and crush.

I was just stepping into a public-house with Travers, when who should drive up but his pretty wife? Most of our friends had paid their adieus at the Surbiton station, but she had driven up by the road in his brougham, bringing their little boy to have a last look at papa. She had also brought his knapsack and greatcoat, and, what was still more acceptable, a basket containing fowls, tongue, bread-and-butter, and biscuits, and a couple of bottles of claret—which priceless luxuries they insisted on my sharing.

Meanwhile the hours went on. The 4th Surrey Militia, which had marched all the way from Kingston,[14] had come up, as well as the other volunteer corps; the station had been partly cleared of the stores that encumbered it; some artillery, two militia regiments, and a battalion of the line, had been despatched, and our turn to start had come, and long lines of carriages were drawn up ready for us; but still we remained in the street.

You may fancy the scene. There seemed to be as many people as ever in London, and we could hardly move for the crowds of spectators—fellows hawking fruits and volunteers' comforts, newsboys and so forth, to say nothing of the cabs and omnibuses; while orderlies and staff officers were constantly riding up with messages. A good many of the militiamen, and some of our people too, had taken more than enough to drink; perhaps a hot sun had told on empty stomachs; anyhow, they became very noisy.

The din, dirt, and heat were indescribable. So the evening wore on, and all the information our officers could get from the brigadier, who

____

[14]Kingston is about 4 miles southwest of London.

appeared to be acting under another general, was that orders had come to stand fast for the present. Gradually the street became quieter and cooler. The brigadier, who, by way of setting an example, had remained for some hours without leaving his saddle, had got a chair out of a shop, and sat nodding in it; most of the men were lying down or sitting on the pavement—some sleeping, some smoking.

In vain had Travers begged his wife to go home. She declared that, having come so far, she would stay and see the last of us. The brougham had been sent away to a by-street, as it blocked up the road; so he sat on a doorstep, she by him on the knapsack. Little Arthur, who had been delighted at the bustle and the uniforms, and in high spirits, became at last very cross, and eventually cried himself to sleep in his father's arms, his golden hair and one little dimpled arm hanging over his shoulder.

Thus went on the weary hours, till suddenly the assembly sounded, and we all started up. We were to return to Waterloo. The landing on the east was only a feint—so ran the rumour— the real attack was on the south. Anything seemed better than indecision and delay, and, tired though we were, the march back was gladly hailed. Mrs. Travers, who made us take the remains of the luncheon with us, we left to look for her carriage; little Arthur, who was awake again, but very good and quiet, in her arms.

WE DID NOT REACH Waterloo till nearly midnight, and there was some delay in starting again. Several volunteer and militia regiments had arrived from the north; the station and all its approaches were jammed up with men, and trains were being despatched away as fast as they could be made up.

All this time no news had reached us since the first announcement; but the excitement then aroused had now passed away under the influence of fatigue and want of sleep, and most of us dozed off as soon as we got under way. I did, at any rate, and was awoke by the train stopping at Leatherhead.

There was an up-train returning to town, and some persons in it were bringing up news from the coast. We could not, from our part of the train, hear what they said, but the rumour was passed up from one carriage to another. The enemy had landed in force at Worthing. Their position had been attacked by the troops from the camp near Brighton, and the action would be renewed in the morning. The volunteers had behaved very well.

This was all the information we could get. So, then, the invasion had come at last. It was clear, at any rate, from what was said, that the enemy had not been driven back yet, and we should be in time most likely to take a share in the defence.

It was sunrise when the train crawled into Dorking,[15] for there had been numerous stoppages on the way; and here it was pulled up for a long time, and we were told to get out and stretch ourselves—an order gladly responded to, for we had been very closely packed all night.

Most of us, too, took the opportunity to make an early breakfast off the food we had brought from Shoreditch. I had the remains of Mrs. Travers's fowl and some bread wrapped up in my waterproof, which I shared with one or two less provident comrades.

We could see from our halting-place that the line was blocked with trains beyond and behind. It must have been about eight o'clock when we got orders to take our seats again, and the train began to move slowly on towards Horsham.[16]

Horsham Junction was the point to be occupied—so the rumour went; but about ten o'clock, when halting at a small station a few miles short of it, the order came to leave the train, and our brigade formed in column on the high road. Beyond us was some field artillery; and

---

[15] Dorking is about 15 miles south of Kingston, so some 20 miles south of London.
[16] Horsham is about 8 miles south of Dorking.

further on, so we were told by a staff officer, another brigade, which was to make up a division with ours.

After more delays the line began to move, but not forwards; our route was towards the northwest, and a sort of suspicion of the state of affairs flashed across my mind. Horsham was already occupied by the enemy's advance guard, and we were to fall back on Leith Common, and take up a position threatening his flank, should he advance either to Guildford or Dorking. This was soon confirmed by what the colonel was told by the brigadier and passed down the ranks; and just now, for the first time, the boom of artillery came up on the light south breeze.

In about an hour the firing ceased. What did it mean? We could not tell. Meanwhile our march continued. The day was very close and sultry, and the clouds of dust stirred up by our feet almost suffocated us. I had saved a soda-water-bottleful of yesterday's claret; but this went only a short way, for there were many mouths to share it with, and the thirst soon became as bad as ever.

Several of the regiment fell out from faintness, and we made frequent halts to rest and let the stragglers come up. At last we reached the top of Leith Hill. It is a striking spot, being the highest point in the south of England. The view from it is splendid, and most lovely did the country look this summer day, although the grass was brown from the long drought.

It was a great relief to get from the dusty road on to the common, and at the top of the hill there was a refreshing breeze. We could see now, for the first time, the whole of our division. Our own regiment did not muster more than 500, for it contained a large number of government office men who had been detained, like Danvers, for duty in town, and others were not much larger; but the militia regiment was very strong, and the whole division, I was told, mustered nearly 5,000 rank and file.

We could see other troops also in extension of our division, and could count a couple of field batteries of Royal Artillery, besides some heavy guns, belonging to the volunteers apparently, drawn by cart horses.

The cooler air, the sense of numbers, and the evident strength of the position we held, raised our spirits, which, I am not ashamed to say, had all the morning been depressed. It was not that we were not eager to close with the enemy, but that the counter-marching and halting ominously betokened a vacillation of purpose in those who had the guidance of affairs. Here in two days the invaders had got more than twenty miles inland, and nothing effectual had been done to stop them. And the ignorance in which we volunteers, from the colonel downwards, were kept of their movements, filled us with uneasiness.

We could not but depict to ourselves the enemy as carrying out all the while firmly his well-considered scheme of attack, and contrasting it with our own uncertainty of purpose. The very silence with which his advance appeared to be conducted filled us with mysterious awe. Meanwhile the day wore on, and we became faint with hunger, for we had eaten nothing since daybreak. No provisions came up, and there were no signs of any commissariat officers.

It seems that when we were at the Waterloo station a whole trainful of provisions was drawn up there, and our colonel proposed that one of the trucks should be taken off and attached to our train, so that we might have some food at hand; but the officer in charge, an assistant controller I think they called him—this control department was a newfangled affair which did us almost as much harm as the enemy in the long run—said his orders were to keep all the stores together, and that he couldn't issue any without authority from the head of his department.

So we had to go without. Those who had tobacco smoked—indeed there is no solace like a pipe under such circumstances. The militia regiment, I heard afterwards, had two days' provisions in their haversacks; it was we volunteers who had no haversacks, and nothing to put in them. All this time, I should tell you, while we were lying on the grass with our arms piled, the general, with the brigadiers and staff, was riding about slowly from point to point of the edge of the common, looking out with his glass towards the south valley.

Orderlies and staff officers were constantly coming, and about three o'clock there arrived up a road that led towards Horsham a small body of lancers and a regiment of yeomanry, who had, it appears, been out in advance, and now drew up a short way in front of us in column facing to the south. Whether they could see anything in their front I could not tell, for we were behind the crest of the hill ourselves, and so could not look into the valley below; but shortly afterwards the assembly sounded. Commanding officers were called out by the general, and received some brief instructions; and the column began to march again towards London, the militia this time coming last in our brigade.

A rumour regarding the object of this countermarch soon spread through the ranks. The enemy was not going to attack us here, but was trying to turn the position on both sides, one column pointing to Reigate, the other to Aldershot; and so we must fall back and take up a position at Dorking. The line of the great chalk range was to be defended. A large force was concentrating at Guildford, another at Reigate, and we should find supports at Dorking.

The enemy would be awaited in these positions. Such, so far as we privates could get at the facts, was to be the plan of operations. Down the hill, therefore, we marched. From one or two points we could catch a brief sight of the railway in the valley below running from Dorking to Horsham. Men in red were working upon it here and there. They were the Royal Engineers, some one said, breaking up the line.

On we marched. The dust seemed worse than ever. In one village through which we passed—I forget the name now—there was a pump on the green. Here we stopped and had a good drink; and passing by a large farm, the farmer's wife and two or three of her maids stood at the gate and handed us hunches of bread and cheese out of some baskets. I got the share of a bit, but the bottom of the good woman's baskets must soon have been reached.

Not a thing else was to be had till we got to Dorking about six o'clock; indeed most of the farmhouses appeared deserted already. On arriving there we were drawn up in the street, and just opposite was a baker's shop. Our fellows asked leave at first by twos and threes to go in and buy some loaves, but soon others began to break off and crowd into the shop, and at last a regular scramble took place. If there had been any order preserved, and a regular distribution arranged, they would no doubt have been steady enough, but hunger makes men selfish; each man felt that his stopping behind would do no good—he would simply lose his share; so it ended by almost the whole regiment joining in the scrimmage, and the shop was cleared out in a couple of minutes; while as for paying, you could not get your hand into your pocket for the crush.

The colonel tried in vain to stop the row; some of the officers were as bad as the men. Just then a staff officer rode by; he could scarcely make way for the crowd, and was pushed against rather rudely, and in a passion he called out to us to behave properly, like soldiers, and not like a parcel of roughs.

"Oh, blow it, governor," said Dick Wake, "you aren't agoing to come between a poor cove and his grub." Wake was an articled attorney, and, as we used to say in those days, a cheeky young chap, although a good-natured fellow enough.

At this speech, which was followed by some more remarks of the sort from those about him, the staff officer became angrier still. "Orderly," cried he to the lancer riding behind him, "take that man to the provost-marshal. As for you, sir," he said, turning to our colonel, who sat on his horse silent with astonishment, "if you don't want some of your men shot before their time, you and your precious officers had better keep this rabble in a little better order"; and poor Dick, who looked crestfallen enough, would certainly have been led off at the tail of the sergeant's horse, if the brigadier had not come up and arranged matters, and marched us off to the hill beyond the town.

This incident made us both angry and crestfallen. We were annoyed at being so roughly spoken to; at the same time we felt we had deserved it, and were ashamed of the misconduct. Then, too, we had lost confidence in our colonel, after the poor figure he cut in the affair. He was a good fellow, the colonel, and showed himself a brave one next day; but he aimed too much at being popular, and didn't understand a bit how to command.

T O RESUME—WE HAD scarcely reached the hill above the town, which we were told was to be our bivouac for the night, when the welcome news came that a food-train had arrived at the station; but there were no carts to bring the things up, so a fatigue party went down and carried back a supply to us in their arms,—loaves, a barrel of rum, packets of tea, and joints of meat— abundance for all; but there was not a kettle or a cooking-pot in the regiment, and we could not eat the meat raw.

The colonel and officers were no better off. They had arranged to have a regular mess, with crockery, steward, and all complete, but the establishment never turned up, and what had become of it no one knew. Some of us were sent back into the town to see what we could procure in the way of cooking utensils. We found the street full of artillery, baggage waggons, and mounted officers, and volunteers shopping like ourselves; and all the houses appeared to be occupied by troops.

We succeeded in getting a few kettles and saucepans, and I obtained for myself a leather bag, with a strap to go over the shoulder, which proved very handy afterwards; and thus laden, we trudged back to our camp on the hill, filling the kettles with dirty water from a little stream which runs between the hill and the town, for there was none to be had above. It was nearly a couple of miles each way; and, exhausted as we were with marching and want of rest, we were almost too tired to eat.

The cooking was of the roughest, as you may suppose; all we could do was to cut off slices of the meat and boil them in the saucepans, using our fingers for forks. The tea, however, was very refreshing; and, thirsty as we were, we drank it by the gallon.

Just before it grew dark, the brigade major came round, and, with the adjutant, showed our colonel how to set a picket in advance of our line a little way down the face of the hill. It was not necessary to place one, I suppose, because the town in our front was still occupied with troops; but no doubt the practice would be usefu We had also a quarter guard, and a line of sentries in front and rear of our line, communicating with those of the regiments on our flanks. Firewood was plentiful, for the hill was covered with beautiful wood; but it took some time to collect it, for we had nothing but our pocket-knives to cut down the branches with.

So we lay down to sleep. My company had no duty, and we had the night undisturbed to ourselves; but, tired though I was, the excitement and the novelty of the situation made sleep difficult. And although the night was still and warm, and we were sheltered by the woods, I soon found it chilly with no better covering than my thin dustcoat, the more so as my clothes, saturated with perspiration during the day, had never dried; and before daylight I woke from a short nap, shivering with cold, and was glad to get warm with others by a fire.

I then noticed that the opposite hills on the south were dotted with fires; and we thought at first they must belong to the enemy, but we were told that the ground up there was still held by a strong rearguard of regulars, and that there need be no fear of a surprise.

A T THE FIRST SIGN of dawn the bugles of the regiments sounded the reveillé, and we were ordered to fall in, and the roll was called. About twenty men were absent, who had fallen out sick the day before; they had been sent up to London by train during the night, I believe.

After standing in column for about half an hour, the brigade major came down with orders to pile arms and stand easy; and perhaps half an hour afterwards we were told to get breakfast as quickly as possible, and to cook a day's food at the same time. This operation was managed pretty much in the same way as the evening before, except that we had our cooking pots and kettles ready.

Meantime there was leisure to look around, and from where we stood there was a commanding view of one of the most beautiful scenes in England. Our regiment was drawn up on the extremity of the ridge which runs from Guildford to Dorking. This is indeed merely a part of the great chalk range which extends from beyond Aldershot east to the Medway; but there is a gap in the ridge just here where the little stream that runs past Dorking turns suddenly to the north, to find its way to the Thames.

We stood on the slope of the hill, as it trends down eastward towards this gap, and had passed our bivouac in what appeared to be a gentleman's park. A little way above us, and to our right, was a very fine country-seat to which the park was attached, now occupied by the headquarters of our division. From this house the hill sloped steeply down southward to the valley below, which runs nearly east and west parallel to the ridge, and carries the railway and the road from Guildford to Reigate; and in which valley, immediately in front of the château, and perhaps a mile and a half distant from it, was the little town of Dorking, nestled in the trees, and rising up the foot of the slopes on the other side of the valley which stretched away to Leith Common, the scene of yesterday's march.

Thus the main part of the town of Dorking was on our right front, but the suburbs stretched away eastward nearly to our proper front, culminating in a small railway station, from which the grassy slopes of the park rose up dotted with shrubs and trees to where we were standing.

Round this railway station was a cluster of villas and one or two mills, of whose gardens we thus had a bird's-eye view, their little ornamental ponds glistening like looking glasses in the morning sun. Immediately on our left the park sloped steeply down to the gap before mentioned, through which ran the little stream, as well as the railway from Epsom to Brighton, nearly due north and south, meeting the Guildford and Reigate line at right angles.

Close to the point of intersection and the little station already mentioned, was the station of the former line where we had stopped the day before. Beyond the gap on the east (our left), and in continuation of our ridge, rose the chalk hill again.

The shoulder of this ridge overlooking the gap is called Box Hill, from the shrubbery of boxwood with which it was covered. Its sides were very steep, and the top of the ridge was covered with troops. The natural strength of our position was manifested at a glance, a high grassy ridge steep to the south, with a stream in front, and but little cover up the sides. It seemed made for a battlefield. The weak point was the gap; the ground at the junction of the railways and the roads immediately at the entrance of the gap formed a little valley, dotted, as I have said, with buildings and gardens. This, in one sense, was the key of the position; for although it would not be tenable while we held the ridge commanding it, the enemy by carrying this point and advancing through the gap would cut our line in two.

But you must not suppose I scanned the ground thus critically at the time. Anybody, indeed, might have been struck with the natural advantages of our position; but what, as I remember, most impressed me, was the peaceful beauty of the scene—the little town with the outline of the houses obscured by a blue mist, the massive crispness of the foliage, the outlines of the great trees, lighted up by the sun, and relieved by deep blue shade. So thick was the timber here, rising up the southern slopes of the valley, that it looked almost as if it might have been a primeval forest.

The quiet of the scene was the more impressive because contrasted in the mind with the scenes we expected to follow; and I can remember as if it were yesterday, the sensation of bitter regret that it should now be too late to avert this coming desecration of our country, which might so easily have been prevented. A little firmness, a little prevision on the part of our rulers, even a little common sense, and this great calamity would have been rendered utterly impossible. Too late, alas! We were like the foolish virgins in the parable.

B UT YOU MUST NOT suppose the scene immediately around was gloomy: the camp was brisk and bustling enough. We had got over the stress of weariness; our stomachs were full; we felt a natural enthusiasm at the prospect of having so soon to take a part as the real defenders of the country, and we were inspirited at the sight of the large force that was now assembled.

Along the slopes which trended off to the rear of our ridge, troops came marching up—volunteers, militia, cavalry, and guns; these, I heard, had come down from the north as far as Leatherhead the night before, and had marched over at daybreak. Long trains, too, began to arrive by the rail through the gap, one after the other, containing militia and volunteers, who moved up to the ridge to the right and left, and took up their position, massed for the most part on the slopes which ran up from, and in rear of, where we stood.

We now formed part of an army corps, we were told, consisting of three divisions, but what regiments composed the other two divisions I never heard. All this movement we could distinctly see from our position, for we had hurried over our breakfast, expecting every minute that the battle would begin, and now stood or sat about on the ground near our piled arms.

Early in the morning, too, we saw a very long train come along the valley from the direction of Guildford, full of redcoats. It halted at the little station at our feet, and the troops alighted. We could soon make out their bear-skins. They were the Guards, coming to reinforce this part of the line. Leaving a detachment of skirmishers to hold the line of the railway embankment, the main body marched up with a springy step and with the band playing, and drew up across the gap on our left, in prolongation of our line. There appeared to be three battalions of them, for they formed up in that number of columns at short intervals.

S HORTLY AFTER THIS I was sent over to Box Hill with a message from our colonel to the colonel of a volunteer regiment stationed there, to know whether an ambulance cart was obtainable, as it was reported this regiment was well supplied with carriage, whereas we were without any; my mission, however, was futile.

Crossing the valley, I found a scene of great confusion at the railway station. Trains were still coming in with stores ammunition, guns, and appliances of all sorts, which were being unloaded as fast as possible; but there were scarcely any means of getting the things off. There were plenty of waggons of all sorts, but hardly any horses to draw them, and the whole place was blocked up; while, to add to the confusion, a regular exodus had taken place of the people from the town, who had been warned that it was likely to be the scene of fighting.

Ladies and women of all sorts and ages, and children, some with bundles, some emptyhanded, were seeking places in the train, but there appeared no one on the spot authorized to grant them, and these poor creatures were pushing their way up and down, vainly asking for information and permission to get away.

In the crowd I observed our surgeon, who likewise was in search of an ambulance of some sort; his whole professional apparatus, he said, consisted of a case of instruments. Also in the crowd I stumbled upon Wood, Travers's old coachman. He had been sent down by his mistress to Guildford, because it was supposed our regiment had gone there, riding the horse, and laden with a supply of things—food, blankets, and, of course, a letter.

He had also brought my knapsack; but at Guildford the horse was pressed for artillery work, and a receipt for it given him in exchange, so he had been obliged to leave all the heavy packages there, including my knapsack; but the faithful old man had brought on as many things as he could carry, and hearing that we should be found in this part, had walked over thus laden from Guildford. He said that place was crowded with troops, and that the heights were lined with them the whole way between the two towns; also, that some trains with wounded had passed up from the coast in the night, through Guildford.

I led him off to where our regiment was, relieving the old man from part of the load he was staggering under. The food sent was not now so much needed, but the plates, knives, etc., and drinking-vessels, promised to be handy—and Travers, you may be sure, was delighted to get his letter; while a couple of newspapers the old man had brought were eagerly competed for by all, even at this critical moment, for we had heard no authentic news since we left London on Sunday.

And even at this distance of time, although I only glanced down the paper, I can remember almost the very words I read there. They were both copies of the same paper: the first, published on Sunday evening, when the news had arrived of the successful landing at three points, was written in a tone of despair. The country must confess that it had been taken by surprise. The conqueror would be satisfied with the humiliation inflicted by a peace dictated on our own shores; it was the clear duty of the government to accept the best terms obtainable, and to avoid further bloodshed and disaster, and avert the fall of our tottering mercantile credit.

The next morning's issue was in quite a different tone. Apparently the enemy had received a check, for we were here exhorted to resistance. An impregnable position was to be taken up along the Downs, a force was concentrating there far outnumbering the rash invaders, who, with an invincible line before them, and the sea behind, had no choice between destruction or surrender. Let there be no pusillanimous talk of negotiation, the fight must be fought out; and there could be but one issue. England, expectant but calm, awaited with confidence the result of the attack on its unconquerable volunteers.

The writing appeared to me eloquent, but rather inconsistent. The same paper said the government had sent off 500 workmen from Woolwich, to open a branch arsenal at Birmingham.

ALL THIS TIME WE had nothing to do, except to change our position, which we did every few minutes, now moving up the hill farther to our right, now taking ground lower down to our left, as one order after another was brought down the line; but the staff officers were galloping about perpetually with orders, while the rumble of the artillery as they moved about from one part of the field to another went on almost incessantly.

At last the whole line stood to arms, the bands struck up, and the general commanding our army corps came riding down with his staff. We had seen him several times before, as we had been moving frequently about the position during the morning; but he now made a sort of formal inspection. He was a tall thin man, with long light hair, very well mounted, and as he sat his horse with an erect seat, and came prancing down the line, at a little distance he looked as if he might be five-and-twenty; but I believe he had served more than fifty years, and had been made a peer for services performed when quite an old man.

I remember that he had more decorations than there was room for on the breast of his coat, and wore them suspended like a necklace round his neck. Like all the other generals, he was dressed in blue, with a cocked hat and feathers—a bad plan, I thought, for it made them very conspicuous.

The general halted before our battalion, and after looking at us a while, made a short address: We had a post of honour next Her Majesty's Guards, and would show ourselves worthy of it, and of the name of Englishmen. It did not need, he said, to be a general to see the strength of our position; it was impregnable, if properly held. Let us wait till the enemy was well pounded, and then the word would be given to go at him. Above everything, we must be steady. He then shook hands with our colonel, we gave him a cheer, and he rode on to where the Guards were drawn up.

NOW THEN, WE THOUGHT, the battle will begin. But still there were no signs of the enemy; and the air, though hot and sultry, began to be very hazy, so that you could scarcely see the town below, and the hills opposite were merely a confused blur, in which no features could be distinctly made out.

After a while, the tension of feeling which followed the general's address relaxed, and we began to feel less as if everything depended on keeping our rifles firmly grasped; we were told to pile arms again, and got leave to go down by tens and twenties to the stream below to drink. This stream, and all the hedges and banks on our side of it, were held by our skirmishers, but the town had been abandoned. The position appeared an excellent one, except that the enemy, when they came, would have almost better cover than our men.

While I was down at the brook, a column emerged from the town, making for our position. We thought for a moment it was the enemy, and you could not make out the colour of the uniforms for the dust; but it turned out to be our rearguard, falling back from the opposite hills which they had occupied the previous night.

One battalion, of rifles, halted for a few minutes at the stream to let the men drink, and I had a minute's talk with a couple of the officers. They had formed part of the force which had attacked the enemy on their first landing. They had it all their own way, they said, at first, and could have beaten the enemy back easily if they had been properly supported; but the whole thing was mismanaged. The volunteers came on very pluckily, they said, but they got into confusion, and so did the militia, and the attack failed with serious loss. It was the wounded of this force which had passed through Guildford in the night. The officers asked us eagerly about the arrangements for the battle, and when we said that the Guards were the only regular troops in this part of the field, shook their heads ominously.

WHILE WE WERE TALKING a third officer came up; he was a dark man with a smooth face and a curious excited manner. "You are volunteers, I suppose," he said, quickly, his eye flashing the while. "Well, now, look here; mind I don't want to hurt your feelings, or to say anything unpleasant, but I'll tell you what; if all you gentlemen were just to go back, and leave us to fight it out alone, it would be a devilish good thing. We could do it a precious deal better without you, I assure you. We don't want your help, I can tell you. We would much rather be left alone, I assure you. Mind I don't want to say anything rude, but that's a fact."

Having blurted out this passionately, he strode away before any one could reply, or the other officers could stop him. They apologized for his rudeness, saying that his brother, also in the regiment, had been killed on Sunday, and that this, and the sun, and marching, had affected his head. The officers told us that the enemy's advance guard was close behind, but that he had apparently been waiting for reinforcements, and would probably not attack in force until noon.

It was, however, nearly three o'clock before the battle began. We had almost worn out the feeling of expectancy. For twelve hours had we been waiting for the coming struggle, till at last it seemed almost as if the invasion were but a bad dream, and the enemy, as yet unseen by us, had no real existence. So far things had not been very different, but for the numbers and for what we had been told, from a Volunteer review on Brighton Downs.

I remember that these thoughts were passing through my mind as we lay down in groups on the grass, some smoking, some nibbling at their bread, some even asleep, when the listless state we had fallen into was suddenly disturbed by a gunshot fired from the top of the hill on our right, close by the big house. It was the first time I had ever heard a shotted gun fired, and although it is fifty years ago, the angry whistle of the shot as it left the gun is in my ears now. The sound was soon to become common enough. We all jumped up at the report, and fell in almost without the word being given, grasping our rifles tightly, and the leading files peering forward to look for the approaching enemy.

This gun was apparently the signal to begin, for now our batteries opened fire all along the line. What they were firing at I could not see, and I am sure the gunners could not see much themselves. I have told you what a haze had come over the air since the morning, and now the smoke from the guns settled like a pall over the hill, and soon we could see little but the men in our ranks, and the outline of some gunners in the battery drawn up next us on the slope on our right. This firing went on, I should think, for nearly a couple of hours, and still there was no reply. We could see the gunners—it was a troop of horse artillery—working away like fury, ramming, loading, and running up with cartridges, the officer in command riding slowly up and down just behind his guns, and peering out with his field glasses into the mist. Once or twice they ceased firing

to let their smoke clear away, but this did not do much good.

For nearly two hours did this go on, and not a shot came in reply. "If a battle is like this," said Dick Wake, who was my next-hand file, "it's mild work, to say the least." The words were hardly uttered when a rattle of musketry was heard in front; our skirmishers were at it, and very soon the bullets began to sing over our heads, and some struck the ground at our feet. Up to this time we had been in column; we were now deployed into line on the ground assigned to us.

From the valley or gap on our left there ran a lane right up the hill almost due west, or along our front. This lane had a thick bank about four feet high, and the greater part of the regiment was drawn up behind it; but a little way up the hill the lane trended back out of the line, so the right of the regiment here left it and occupied the open grassland of the park. The bank had been cut away at this point to admit of our going in and out. We had been told in the morning to cut down the bushes on the top of the bank, so as to make the space clear for firing over, but we had no tools to work with; however, a party of sappers had come down and finished the job.

My company was on the right, and was thus beyond the shelter of the friendly bank. On our right again was the battery of artillery already mentioned; then came a battalion of the line, then more guns, then a great mass of militia and volunteers and a few line up to the big house. At least this was the order before the firing began; after that I do not know what changes took place.

A ND NOW THE ENEMY'S artillery began to open; where their guns were posted we could not see, but we began to hear the rush of the shells over our heads, and the bang as they burst just beyond. And now what took place I can really hardly tell you. Sometimes when I try and recall the scene, it seems as if it lasted for only a few minutes; yet I know, as we lay on the ground,

I thought the hours would never pass away, as we watched the gunners still plying their task, firing at the invisible enemy, never stopping for a moment except when now and again a dull blow would be heard and a man fall down, then three or four of his comrades would carry him to the rear.

The captain no longer rode up and down; what had become of him I do not know. Two of the guns ceased firing for a time; they had got injured in some way, and up rode an artillery general. I think I see him now, a very handsome man, with straight features and a dark moustache, his breast covered with medals. He appeared in a great rage at the guns stopping fire.

"Who commands this battery?" he cried.

"I do, Sir Henry," said an officer, riding forward, whom I had not noticed before.

The group is before me at this moment, standing out clear against the background of smoke, Sir Henry erect on his splendid charger, his flashing eye, his left arm pointing towards the enemy to enforce something he was going to say, the young officer reining in his horse just beside him, and saluting with his right hand raised to his busby. This for a moment, then a dull thud, and both horses and riders are prostrate on the ground. A round-shot had struck all four at the saddleline. Some of the gunners ran up to help, but neither officer could have lived many minutes.

This was not the first I saw killed. Some time before this, almost immediately on the enemy's artillery opening, as we were lying, I heard something like the sound of metal striking metal, and at the same moment Dick Wake, who was next me in the ranks, leaning on his elbows, sank forward on his face. I looked round and saw what had happened; a shot fired at a high elevation, passing over his head, had struck the ground behind, nearly cutting his thigh off. It must have been the ball striking his sheathed bayonet which made the noise.

Three of us carried the poor fellow to the rear, with difficulty for the shattered limb; but he was nearly dead from loss of blood when we got to the doctor, who was waiting in a sheltered hollow about two hundred yards in rear, with two other doctors in plain clothes, who had come up to help. We deposited our burden and returned to the front. Poor Wake was sensible when we left him, but apparently too shaken by the shock to be able to speak. Wood was there helping the doctors. I paid more visits to the rear of the same sort before the evening was over.

ALL THIS TIME WE were lying there to be fired at without returning a shot, for our skirmishers were holding the line of walls and enclosures below. However, the bank protected most of us, and the brigadier now ordered our right company, which was in the open, to get behind it also; and there we lay about four deep, the shells crashing and bullets whistling over our heads, but hardly a man being touched.[17] Our colonel was, indeed, the only one exposed, for he rode up and down the lane at a footpace as steady as a rock; but he made the major and adjutant dismount, and take shelter behind the hedge, holding their horses. We were all pleased to see him so cool, and it restored our confidence in him, which had been shaken yesterday.

The time seemed interminable while we lay thus inactive. We could not, of course, help peering over the bank to try and see what was going on; but there was nothing to be made out, for now a tremendous thunder-storm, which had been gathering all day, burst on us, and a torrent of almost blinding rain came down, which obscured the view even more than the smoke, while the crashing of the thunder and the glare of the lightning could be heard and seen even above the roar and flashing of the artillery.

---

[17] For infantry, the chief distinction between Napoleonic warfare and the proto-industrial warfare of the 1860s and 1870s was the amount of hot metal in the air. Changes in warfare put cover and concealment at a premium and discouraged approaching the enemy in close order. In the "storm of steel" of industrial warfare, the infantryman's most favored tool is a shovel.

Once the mist lifted, and I saw for a minute an attack on Box Hill, on the other side of the gap on our left. It was like the scene at a theatre—a curtain of smoke all round and a clear gap in the centre, with a sudden gleam of evening sunshine lighting it up.

The steep smooth slope of the hill was crowded with the dark-blue figures of the enemy, whom I now saw for the first time—an irregular outline in front, but very solid in rear: the whole body was moving forward by fits and starts, the men firing and advancing, the officers waving their swords, the columns closing up and gradually making way. Our people were almost concealed by the bushes at the top, whence the smoke and their fire could be seen proceeding; presently from these bushes on the crest came out a red line, and dashed down the brow of the hill, a flame of fire belching out from the front as it advanced. The enemy hesitated, gave way, and finally ran back in a confused crowd down the hill. Then the mist covered the scene, but the glimpse of this splendid charge was inspiriting, and I hoped we should show the same coolness when it came to our turn.

It was about this time that our skirmishers fell back, a good many wounded, some limping along by themselves, others helped. The main body retired in very fair order, halting to turn round and fire; we could see a mounted officer of the Guards riding up and down encouraging them to be steady. Now came our turn. For a few minutes we saw nothing, but a rattle of bullets came through the rain and mist, mostly, however, passing over the bank. We began to fire in reply, stepping up against the bank to fire, and stooping down to load; but our brigade major rode up with an order, and the word was passed through the men to reserve our fire.[18]

In a very few moments it must have been that,

when ordered to stand up, we could see the helmet spikes and then the figures of the skirmishers as they came on[19]; a lot of them there appeared to be, five or six deep I should say, but in loose order, each man stopping to aim and fire, and then coming forward a little. Just then the brigadier clattered on horseback up the lane.

"Now then, gentlemen, give it them hot!" he cried; and fire away we did, as fast as ever we were able. A perfect storm of bullets seemed to be flying about us too, and I thought each moment must be the last; escape seemed impossible, but I saw no one fall, for I was too busy, and so were we all, to look to the right or left, but loaded and fired as fast as we could.

How long this went on I know not—it could not have been long; neither side could have lasted many minutes under such a fire, but it ended by the enemy gradually falling back, and as soon as we saw this we raised a tremendous shout, and some of us jumped up on the bank to give them our parting shots. Suddenly the order was passed down the line to cease firing, and we soon discovered the cause; a battalion of the Guards was charging obliquely across from our left across our front. It was, I expect, their flank attack as much as our fire which had turned back the enemy; and it was a splendid sight to see their steady line as they advanced slowly across the smooth lawn below us, firing as they went, but as steady as if on parade. We felt a great elation at this moment; it seemed as if the battle was won.

Just then somebody called out to look to the wounded, and for the first time I turned to glance down the rank along the lane. Then I saw that we had not beaten back the attack without loss. Immediately before me lay Bob Lawford of my office, dead on his back from a bullet through his forehead, his hand still grasping his rifle. At every step was some friend or acquaintance killed or

---

[18] It is no coincidence that the British Army began a transition from the single-shot, muzzle-loading Snider-Enfield rifle to the breech-loading Martini-Henry in 1871. The Dreyse needle gun, in wide service in the Prussian Army at the time, was a breech-loading bolt-action rifle that fired six rounds per minute. Similarly, the French *chassepot* rifle fired 8–15 rounds per minute. Chesney is here likely describing single-shot, muzzle loading rifles that could fire about three rounds per minute.

[19] Helmet spikes characterized Imperial German field dress until World War I.

wounded, and a few paces down the lane I found Travers, sitting with his back against the bank. A ball had gone through his lungs, and blood was coming from his mouth.

I was lifting him up, but the cry of agony he gave stopped me. I then saw that this was not his only wound; his thigh was smashed by a bullet (which must have hit him when standing on the bank), and the blood streaming down mixed in a muddy puddle with the rainwater under him. Still he could not be left here, so, lifting him up as well as I could, I carried him through the gate which led out of the lane at the back to where our camp hospital was in the rear. The movement must have caused him awful agony, for I could not support the broken thigh, and he could not restrain his groans, brave fellow though he was; but how I carried him at all I cannot make out, for he was a much bigger man than myself; but I had not gone far, one of a stream of our fellows, all on the same errand, when a bandsman and Wood met me, bringing a hurdle as a stretcher, and on this we placed him.

Wood had just time to tell me that he had got a cart down in the hollow, and would endeavour to take off his master at once to Kingston, when a staff-officer rode up to call us to the ranks. "You really must not straggle in this way, gentlemen," he said; "pray keep your ranks."

"But we can't leave our wounded to be trodden down and die," cried one of our fellows.

"Beat off the enemy first, sir," he replied. "Gentlemen, do, pray, join your regiments, or we shall be a regular mob."

And no doubt he did not speak too soon; for besides our fellows straggling to the rear, lots of volunteers from the regiments in reserve were running forward to help, till the whole ground was dotted with groups of men. I hastened back to my post, but I had just time to notice that all the ground in our rear was occupied by a thick mass of troops, much more numerous than in the morning, and a column was moving down to the left of our line, to the ground before held by the Guards. All this time, although musketry had slackened, the artillery fire seemed heavier than ever; the shells screamed overhead or burst around; and I confess to feeling quite a relief at getting back to the friendly shelter of the lane.[20]

Looking over the bank, I noticed for the first time the frightful execution our fire had created. The space in front was thickly strewed with dead and badly wounded, and beyond the bodies of the fallen enemy could just be seen—for it was now getting dusk—the bear-skins and red coats of our own gallant Guards scattered over the slope, and marking the line of their victorious advance.

But hardly a minute could have passed in thus looking over the field, when our brigade major came moving up the lane on foot (I suppose his horse had been shot), crying, "Stand to your arms, volunteers! They're coming on again," and we found ourselves a second time engaged in a hot musketry fire.

How long it went on I cannot now remember, but we could distinguish clearly the thick line of skirmishers, about sixty paces off and mounted officers among them; and we seemed to be keeping them well in check, for they were quite exposed to our fire, while we were protected nearly up to our shoulders, when—I know not how—I became sensible that something had gone wrong.

"We are taken in flank!" called out someone; and looking along the left, sure enough there were dark figures jumping over the bank into the lane and firing up along our line. The volunteers in reserve, who had come down to take the place of the Guards, must have given way at this point; the enemy's skirmishers had got through our line, and turned our left flank.

How the next move came about I cannot recollect, or whether it was without orders, but in a short time we found ourselves out of the lane, and drawn up in a straggling line about thirty yards

---

[20]This suggests the increasing role of artillery on the battlefield at the time. Most speculative military fiction relies on either medieval or futuristic technology, so it is nice to have a story involving proto-industrial technology.

in rear of it—at our end, that is, the other flank had fallen back a good deal more—and the enemy were lining the hedge, and numbers of them passing over and forming up on our side. Beyond our left a confused mass were retreating, firing as they went, followed by the advancing line of the enemy. We stood in this way for a short space, firing at random as fast as we could.

Our colonel and major must have been shot, for there was no one to give an order, when somebody on horseback called out from behind—I think it must have been the brigadier—"Now, then, volunteers! Give a British cheer, and go at them—charge!" and, with a shout, we rushed at the enemy. Some of them ran, some stopped to meet us, and for a moment it was a real hand-to-hand fight. I felt a sharp sting in my leg, as I drove my bayonet right through the man in front of me. I confess I shut my eyes, for I just got a glimpse of the poor wretch as he fell back, his eyes starting out of his head, and, savage though we were, the sight was almost too horrible to look at.

But the struggle was over in a second, and we had cleared the ground again right up to the rear hedge of the lane. Had we gone on, I believe we might have recovered the lane too, but we were now all out of order; there was no one to say what to do; the enemy began to line the hedge and open fire, and they were streaming past our left; and how it came about I know not, but we found ourselves falling back towards our right rear, scarce any semblance of a line remaining, and the volunteers who had given way on our left mixed up with us, and adding to the confusion.

It was now nearly dark. On the slopes which we were retreating to was a large mass of reserves drawn up in columns. Some of the leading files of these, mistaking us for the enemy, began firing at us; our fellows, crying out to them to stop, ran towards their ranks, and in a few moments the whole slope of the hill became a scene of confusion that I cannot attempt to describe, regiments and detachments mixed up in hopeless disorder. Most of us, I believe, turned towards

the enemy and fired away our few remaining cartridges; but it was too late to take aim, fortunately for us, or the guns which the enemy had brought up through the gap, and were firing point-blank, would have done more damage.

As it was, we could see little more than the bright flashes of their fire. In our confusion we had jammed up a line regiment immediately behind us, which I suppose had just arrived on the field, and its colonel and some staff officers were in vain trying to make a passage for it, and their shouts to us to march to the rear and clear a road could be heard above the roar of the guns and the confused babel of sound.

At last a mounted officer pushed his way through, followed by a company in sections, the men brushing past with firm-set faces, as if on a desperate task; and the battalion, when it got clear, appeared to deploy and advance down the slope. I have also a dim recollection of seeing the Life Guards trot past the front, and push on towards the town—a last desperate attempt to save the day—before we left the field.

Our adjutant, who had got separated from our flank of the regiment in the confusion, now came up, and managed to lead us, or at any rate some of us, up to the crest of the hill in the rear, to re-form, as he said; but there we met a vast crowd of volunteers, militia, and waggons, all hurrying rearward from the direction of the big house, and we were borne in the stream for a mile at least before it was possible to stop. At last the adjutant led us to an open space a little off the line of fugitives, and there we re-formed the remains of the companies. Telling us to halt, he rode off to try and obtain orders, and find out where the rest of our brigade was.

From this point, a spur of high ground running off from the main plateau, we looked down through the dim twilight into the battlefield below. Artillery-fire was still going on. We could see the flashes from the guns on both sides, and now and then a stray shell came screaming up and burst near us, but we were beyond the sound of musketry. This halt first gave us time to think about what had happened. The long day of expectancy had been succeeded by the excitement of battle; and when each minute may be your last, you do not think much about other people, nor when you are facing another man with a rifle have you time to consider whether he or you are the invader, or that you are fighting for your home and hearths.

All fighting is pretty much alike, I suspect, as to sentiment, when once it begins. But now we had time for reflection; and although we did not yet quite understand how far the day had gone against us, an uneasy feeling of self-condemnation must have come up in the minds of most of us; while, above all, we now began to realise what the loss of this battle meant to the country. Then, too, we knew not what had become of all our wounded comrades. Reaction, too, set in after the fatigue and excitement. For myself, I had found out for the first time that besides the bayonet wound in my leg, a bullet had gone through my left arm, just below the shoulder, and outside the bone. I remember feeling something like a blow just when we lost the lane, but the wound passed unnoticed till now, when the bleeding had stopped and the shirt was sticking to the wound.

THIS HALF HOUR SEEMED an age, and while we stood on this knoll the endless tramp of men and rumbling of carts along the downs beside us told their own tale. The whole army was falling back. At last we could discern the adjutant riding up to us out of the dark. The army was to retreat and take up a position on Epsom Downs,[21] he said; we should join in the march, and try and find our brigade in the morning; and so we turned into the throng again, and made our way on as best we could.

A few scraps of news he gave us as he rode alongside of our leading section; the army had

held its position well for a time, but the enemy had at last broken through the line between us and Guildford, as well as in our front, and had poured his men through the point gained, throwing the line into confusion, and the first army corps near Guildford were also falling back to avoid being outflanked. The regular troops were holding the rear; we were to push on as fast as possible to get out of their way, and allow them to make an orderly retreat in the morning. The gallant old lord commanding our corps had been badly wounded early in the day, he heard, and carried off the field. The Guards had suffered dreadfully; the household cavalry had ridden down the cuirassiers, but had got into broken ground and been awfully cut up. Such were the scraps of news passed down our weary column.

What had become of our wounded no one knew, and no one liked to ask. So we trudged on.

It must have been midnight when we reached Leatherhead. Here we left the open ground and took to the road, and the block became greater. We pushed our way painfully along; several trains passed slowly ahead along the railway by the roadside, containing the wounded, we supposed—such of them, at least, as were lucky enough to be picked up.

It was daylight when we got to Epsom. The night had been bright and clear after the storm, with a cool air, which, blowing through my soaking clothes, chilled me to the bone. My wounded leg was stiff and sore, and I was ready to drop with exhaustion and hunger. Nor were my comrades in much better case; we had eaten nothing since breakfast the day before, and the bread we had put by had been washed away by the storm: only a little pulp remained at the bottom of my bag. The tobacco was all too wet to smoke.

In this plight we were creeping along, when the adjutant guided us into a field by the roadside to rest awhile, and we lay down exhausted on the sloppy grass. The roll was here taken, and only 180 answered out of nearly 500 present on

____

[21] Epson Downs is about halfway between Dorking and Kingston.

the morning of the battle. How many of these were killed and wounded no one could tell; but it was certain many must have got separated in the confusion of the evening.

While resting here, we saw pass by, in the crowd of vehicles and men, a cart laden with commissariat stores, driven by a man in uniform. "Food!" cried someone, and a dozen volunteers jumped up and surrounded the cart. The driver tried to whip them off; but he was pulled off his seat, and the contents of the cart thrown out in an instant. They were preserved meats in tins, which we tore open with our bayonets. The meat had been cooked before, I think; at any rate we devoured it. Shortly after this a general came by with three or four staff officers. He stopped and spoke to our adjutant, and then rode into the field. "My lads," said he, "you shall join my division for the present: fall in, and follow the regiment that is now passing."

We rose up, fell in by companies, each about twenty strong, and turned once more into the stream moving along the road—regiments, detachments, single volunteers or militiamen, country people making off, some with bundles, some without, a few in carts, but most on foot; here and there waggons of stores, with men sitting wherever there was room, others crammed with wounded soldiers. Many blocks occurred from horses falling, or carts breaking down and filling up the road.

In the town the confusion was even worse, for all the houses seemed full of volunteers and militiamen, wounded, or resting, or trying to find food, and the streets were almost choked up. Some officers were in vain trying to restore order, but the task seemed a hopeless one. One or two volunteer regiments which had arrived from the north the previous night, and had been halted here for orders, were drawn up along the roadside steadily enough, and some of the retreating regiments, including ours, may have preserved the semblance of discipline, but for the most part the mass pushing to the rear was a mere mob. The regulars, or what remained of them, were now, I believe, all in

the rear, to hold the advancing enemy in check. A few officers among such a crowd could do nothing.

To add to the confusion several houses were being emptied of the wounded brought here the night before, to prevent their falling into the hands of the enemy, some in carts, some being carried to the railway by men. The groans of these poor fellows as they were jostled through the street went to our hearts, selfish though fatigue and suffering had made us.

At last, following the guidance of a staff officer who was standing to show the way, we turned off from the main London road and took that towards Kingston. Here the crush was less, and we managed to move along pretty steadily. The air had been cooled by the storm, and there was no dust. We passed through a village where our new general had seized all the public houses, and taken possession of the liquor; and each regiment as it came up was halted, and each man got a drink of beer, served out by companies. Whether the owner got paid, I know not, but it was like nectar.

It must have been about one o'clock in the afternoon that we came in sight of Kingston. We had been on our legs sixteen hours, and had got over about twelve miles of ground. There is a hill a little south of the Surbiton station, covered then mostly with villas, but open at the western extremity, where there was a clump of trees on the summit. We had diverged from the road towards this, and here the general halted us and disposed the line of the division along his front, facing to the south-west, the right of the line reaching down to the waterworks on the Thames, the left extending along the southern slope of the hill, in the direction of the Epsom road by which we had come. We were nearly in the centre, occupying the knoll just in front of the general, who dismounted on the top and tied his horse to a tree.

It is not much of a hill, but commands an extensive view over the flat country around; and as we lay wearily on the ground we could see the Thames glistening like a silver field in the bright sunshine, the palace at Hampton Court, the bridge at Kingston, and the old church tower rising above the haze of the town, with the woods of Richmond Park behind it. To most of us the scene could not but call up the associations of happy days of peace—days now ended and peace destroyed through national infatuation. We did not say this to each other, but a deep depression had come upon us, partly due to weakness and fatigue, no doubt, but we saw that another stand was going to be made, and we had no longer any confidence in ourselves. If we could not hold our own when stationary in line, on a good position, but had been broken up into a rabble at the first shock, what chance had we now of manoeuvring against a victorious enemy in this open ground?

A feeling of desperation came over us, a determination to struggle on against hope; but anxiety for the future of the country, and our friends, and all dear to us, filled our thoughts now that we had time for reflection. We had had no news of any kind since Wood joined us the day before—we knew not what was doing in London, or what the government was about, or anything else; and exhausted though we were, we felt an intense craving to know what was happening in other parts of the country.

Our general had expected to find a supply of food and ammunition here, but nothing turned up. Most of us had hardly a cartridge left, so he ordered the regiment next to us, which came from the north and had not been engaged, to give us enough to make up twenty rounds a man, and he sent off a fatigue party to Kingston to try and get provisions, while a detachment of our fellows was allowed to go foraging among the villas in our rear; and in about an hour they brought back some bread and meat, which gave us a slender meal all round. They said most of the houses were empty, and that many had been stripped of all eatables, and a good deal damaged already.

I T MUST HAVE BEEN between three and four o'clock when the sound of cannonading began to be heard in the front, and we could see the smoke of the guns rising above the woods of Esher and Claremont, and soon afterwards some troops emerged from the fields below us. It was the rearguard of regular troops. There were some guns also, which were driven up the slope and took up their position round the knoll. There were three batteries, but they only counted eight guns amongst them.[22] Behind them was posted the line; it was a brigade apparently of four regiments, but the whole did not look to be more than eight or nine hundred men. Our regiment and another had been moved a little to the rear to make way for them, and presently we were ordered down to occupy the railway station on our right rear.

My leg was now so stiff I could no longer march with the rest, and my left arm was very swollen and sore, and almost useless; but anything seemed better than being left behind, so I limped after the battalion as best I could down to the station. There was a goods shed a little in advance of it down the line, a strong brick building, and here my company was posted. The rest of our men lined the wall of the enclosure.

A staff officer came with us to arrange the distribution; we should be supported by line troops, he said; and in a few minutes a train full of them came slowly up from Guildford way. It was the last; the men got out, the train passed on, and a party began to tear up the rails, while the rest were distributed among the houses on each side. A sergeant's party joined us in our shed, and an engineer officer with sappers came to knock holes in the walls for us to fire from; but there

---

[22]Artillery batteries usually consisted of about six guns at this time (around eighteen guns across three batteries), so this represents attrition of over 50 percent.

were only half-a-dozen of them, so progress was not rapid, and as we had no tools we could not help.

It was while we were watching this job that the adjutant, who was as active as ever, looked in, and told us to muster in the yard. The fatigue party had come back from Kingston, and a small baker's hand-cart of food was made over to us as our share. It contained loaves, flour, and some joints of meat. The meat and the flour we had not time or means to cook. The loaves we devoured; and there was a tap of water in the yard, so we felt refreshed by the meal.

I should have liked to wash my wounds, which were becoming very offensive, but I dared not take off my coat, feeling sure I should not be able to get it on again. It was while we were eating our bread that the rumour first reached us of another disaster, even greater than that we had witnessed ourselves. Whence it came I know not; but a whisper went down the ranks that Woolwich had been captured. We all knew that it was our only arsenal, and understood the significance of the blow. No hope, if this were true, of saving the country. Thinking over this, we went back to the shed.

ALTHOUGH THIS WAS ONLY our second day of war, I think we were already old soldiers so far that we had come to be careless about fire, and the shot and shell that now began to open on us made no sensation. We felt, indeed, our need of discipline, and we saw plainly enough the slender chance of success coming out of troops so imperfectly trained as we were; but I think we were all determined to fight on as long as we could.

Our gallant adjutant gave his spirit to everybody; and the staff officer commanding was a very cheery fellow, and went about as if we were certain of victory. Just as the firing began he looked in to say that we were as safe as in a church, that we must be sure and pepper the enemy well, and

that more cartridges would soon arrive. There were some steps and benches in the shed, and on these a party of our men were standing, to fire through the upper loopholes, while the line soldiers and others stood on the ground, guarding the second row. I sat on the floor, for I could not now use my rifle, and besides, there were more men than loopholes.

The artillery fire which had opened now on our position was from a longish range; and occupation for the riflemen had hardly begun when there was a crash in the shed, and I was knocked down by a blow on the head. I was almost stunned for a time, and could not make out at first what had happened. A shot or shell had hit the shed without quite penetrating the wall, but the blow had upset the steps resting against it, and the men standing on them, bringing down a cloud of plaster and brickbats, one of which had struck me.

I felt now past being of use. I could not use my rifle, and could barely stand; and after a time I thought I would make for my own house, on the chance of finding some one still there. I got up therefore, and staggered homewards. Musketry fire had now commenced, and our side were blazing away from the windows of the houses, and from behind walls, and from the shelter of some trucks still standing in the station. A couple of field-pieces in the yard were firing, and in the open space in rear of the station a reserve was drawn up. There, too, was the staff officer on horseback, watching the fight through his field glass.

I remember having still enough sense to feel that the position was a hopeless one. That straggling line of houses and gardens would surely be broken through at some point, and then the line must give way like a rope of sand. It was about a mile to our house, and I was thinking how I could possibly drag myself so far when I suddenly recollected that I was passing Travers's house—one of the first of a row of villas then leading from the Surbiton station to Kingston. Had he been brought home, I wondered, as his faithful old servant promised, and was his wife still here?

I remember to this day the sensation of shame I felt, when I recollected that I had not once given him—my greatest friend—a thought since I carried him off the field the day before. But war and suffering make men selfish. I would go in now at any rate and rest awhile, and see if I could be of use. The little garden before the house was as trim as ever—I used to pass it every day on my way to the train, and knew every shrub in it—and ablaze with flowers, but the hall-door stood ajar.

I stepped in and saw little Arthur standing in the hall. He had been dressed as neatly as ever that day, and as he stood there in his pretty blue frock and white trousers and socks showing his chubby little legs, with his golden locks, fair face, and large dark eyes, the picture of childish beauty, in the quiet hall, just as it used to look— the vases of flowers, the hat and coats hanging up, the familiar pictures on the walls—this vision of peace in the midst of war made me wonder for a moment, faint and giddy as I was, if the pandemonium outside had any real existence, and was not merely a hideous dream. But the roar of the guns making the house shake, and the rushing of the shot, gave a ready answer.

The little fellow appeared almost unconscious of the scene around him, and was walking up the stairs holding by the railing, one step at a time, as I had seen him do a hundred times before, but turned round as I came in. My appearance frightened him, and staggering as I did into the hall, my face and clothes covered with blood and dirt, I must have looked an awful object to the child, for he gave a cry and turned to run toward the basement stairs. But he stopped on hearing my voice calling him back to his god-papa, and after a while came timidly up to me. Papa had been to the battle, he said, and was very ill; mamma was with papa; Wood was out; Lucy was in the cellar, and had taken him there, but he wanted to go to mamma. Telling him to stay in the hall for a minute till I called him, I climbed upstairs and opened the bedroom door.

My poor friend lay there, his body resting on the bed, his head supported on his wife's shoulder as she sat by the bedside. He breathed heavily, but the pallor of his face, the closed eyes, the prostrate arms, the clammy foam she was wiping from his mouth, all spoke of approaching death. The good old servant had done his duty, at least—he had brought his master home to die in his wife's arms. The poor woman was too intent on her charge to notice the opening of the door and as the child would be better away, I closed it gently and went down to the hall to take little Arthur to the shelter below, where the maid was hiding.

Too late! He lay at the foot of the stairs on his face, his little arms stretched out, his hair dabbled in blood. I had not noticed the crash among the other noises, but a splinter of a shell must have come through the open doorway; it had carried away the back of his head. The poor child's death must have been instantaneous. I tried to lift up the little corpse with my one arm, but even this load was too much for me, and while stooping down I fainted away.

WHEN I CAME TO my senses again it was quite dark, and for some time I could not make out where I was; I lay indeed for some time like one half asleep, feeling no inclination to move. By degrees I became aware that I was on the carpeted floor of a room. All noise of battle had ceased, but there was a sound as of many people close by. At last I sat up and gradually got to my feet. The movement gave me intense pain, for my wounds were now highly inflamed, and my clothes sticking to them made them dreadfully sore.

At last I got up and groped my way to the door, and opening it at once saw where I was, for the pain had brought back my senses. I had been lying in Travers's little writing room at the end of the passage, into which I made my way. There was no gas, and the drawing room door was closed; but from the open dining room the glimmer of a candle feebly lighted up the hall, in which half-a-dozen sleeping figures could be discerned, while the room itself was crowded with men. The table was covered with plates, glasses, and bottles; but most of the men were asleep in the chairs or on the floor, a few were smoking cigars, and one or two with their helmets on were still engaged at supper, occasionally grunting out an observation between the mouthfuls.

"*Sind wackere Soldaten, diese Englischen Freiwilligen,*" said a broad-shouldered brute, stuffing a great hunch of beef into his mouth with a silver fork, an implement I should think he must have been using for the first time in his life.[23]

"*Ja, ja,*" replied a comrade, who was lolling back in his chair with a pair of very dirty legs on the table, and one of poor Travers's best cigars in his mouth. "*Sie so gut laufen können.*"

"*Ja wohl,*" responded the first speaker. "*Aber sind nicht eben so schnell wie die Französischen Mobloten.*"

"*Gewiss,*" grunted a hulking lout from the floor, leaning on his elbow, and sending out a cloud of smoke from his ugly jaws, "*und da sind hier etwa gute Schützen.*"

"*Hast recht, lange Peter,*" answered number one. "*Wenn die Schurken so gut exerciren wie schützen könnten, so wären wir heute nicht hier!*"

"*Recht! Recht!*" said the second. "*Das exerciren macht den guten Soldaten.*"

WHAT MORE CRITICISMS X ON the shortcomings of our unfortunate volunteers might have passed I did not stop to hear, being interrupted by a sound on the stairs. Mrs. Travers was standing on the landing place; I limped up the stairs to meet her. Among the many pictures of those fatal days engraven on my memory, I remember none more clearly than the mournful aspect of my poor friend, widowed and childless

within a few moments, as she stood there in her white dress, coming forth like a ghost from the chamber of the dead, the candle she held lighting up her face, and contrasting its pallor with the dark hair that fell disordered round it, its beauty radiant even through features worn with fatigue and sorrow.

She was calm and even tearless, though the trembling lip told of the effort to restrain the emotion she felt. "Dear friend," she said, taking my hand, "I was coming to seek you; forgive my selfishness in neglecting you so long; but you will understand"—glancing at the door above—"how occupied I have been."

"Where," I began, "is—"

"My boy?" she answered, anticipating my question. "I have laid him by his father. But now your wounds must be cared for; how pale and faint you look! Rest here a moment." And, descending to the dining-room, she returned with some wine, which I gratefully drank, and then, making me sit down on the top step of the stairs, she brought water and linen, and, cutting off the sleeve of my coat, bathed and bandaged my wounds. 'Twas I who felt selfish for thus adding to her troubles; but in truth I was too weak to have much will left, and stood in need of the help which she forced me to accept; and the dressing of my wounds afforded indescribable relief.

While thus tending me, she explained in broken sentences how matters stood. Every room but her own, and the little parlour into which with Wood's help she had carried me, was full of soldiers. Wood had been taken away to work at repairing the railroad and Lucy had run off from fright; but the cook had stopped at her post, and had served up supper and opened the cellar for the soldiers' use; she herself did not understand what they said, and they were rough and boorish, but not uncivil. I should now go, she said, when my wounds were dressed, to look after my own home, where I might be wanted; for herself, she

---

[23]In this conversation, the Prussian soldiers comment on the quality and marksmanship of the English volunteers, while remarking that if they were better trained the Prussians wouldn't have gotten this far.

wished only to be allowed to remain watching there—glancing at the room where lay the bodies of her husband and child—where she would not be molested.

I felt that her advice was good. I could be of no use as protection, and I had an anxious longing to know what had become of my sick mother and sister; besides, some arrangement must be made for the burial. I therefore limped away. There was no need to express thanks on either side, and the grief was too deep to be reached by any outward show of sympathy.

OUTSIDE THE HOUSE THERE was a good deal of movement and bustle; many carts going along, the waggoners, from Sussex and Surrey, evidently impressed and guarded by soldiers; and although no gas was burning, the road towards Kingston was well lighted by torches held by persons standing at short intervals in line, who had been seized for the duty, some of them the tenants of neighbouring villas.

Almost the first of these torchbearers I came to was an old gentleman whose face I was well acquainted with, from having frequently travelled up and down in the same train with him. He was a senior clerk in a government office, I believe, and was a mild-looking old man with a prim face and a long neck, which he used to wrap in a white double neckcloth, a thing even in those days seldom seen. Even in that moment of bitterness I could not help being amused by the absurd figure this poor old fellow presented, with his solemn face and long cravat doing penance with a torch in front of his own gate, to light up the path of our conquerors.

But a more serious object now presented itself, a corporal's guard passing by, with two English volunteers in charge, their hands tied behind their backs. They cast an imploring glance at me, and I stepped into the road to ask the corporal what was the matter, and even ventured, as he was passing on, to lay my hand on his sleeve.

"*Auf dem Wege, Spitzbube!*" cried the brute, lifting his rifle as if to knock me down. "Must one prisoners who fire at us let shoot," he went on to add; and shot the poor fellows would have been, I suppose, if I had not interceded with an officer, who happened to be riding by.

"*Herr Hauptmann,*" I cried, as loud as I could, "is this your discipline, to let unarmed prisoners be shot without orders?"

The officer, thus appealed to, reined in his horse, and halted the guard till he heard what I had to say. My knowledge of other languages here stood me in good stead, for the prisoners, north country factory hands apparently, were of course utterly unable to make themselves understood, and did not even know in what they had offended. I therefore interpreted their explanation; they had been left behind while skirmishing near Ditton, in a barn, and coming out of their hiding place in the midst of a party of the enemy, with their rifles in their hands, the latter thought they were going to fire at them from behind. It was a wonder they were not shot down on the spot. The captain heard the tale, and then told the guard to let them go, and they slunk off at once into a by-road.

He was a fine soldier-like man, but nothing could exceed the insolence of his manner, which was perhaps all the greater because it seemed not intentional, but to arise from a sense of immeasurable superiority. Between the lame *freiwilliger* pleading for his comrades, and the captain of the conquering army, there was, in his view, an infinite gulf. Had the two men been dogs, their fate could not have been decided more contemptuously. They were let go simply because they were not worth keeping as prisoners, and perhaps to kill any living thing without cause went against the *hauptmann's* sense of justice.

But why speak of this insult in particular? Had not every man who lived then his tale to tell of humiliation and degradation? For it was the same story everywhere. After the first stand in line, and when once they had got us on the march, the enemy laughed at us. Our handful of regular troops was sacrificed almost to a man in a vain conflict with numbers; our volunteers and militia, with officers who did not know their work, without ammunition or equipment, or staff to superintend, starving in the midst of plenty, we had soon become a helpless mob, fighting desperately here and there, but with whom, as a manoeuvring army, the disciplined invaders did just what they pleased.

H APPY THOSE WHOSE BONES whitened the fields of Surrey; they at least were spared the disgrace we lived to endure. Even you, who have never known what it is to live otherwise than on sufferance, even your cheeks burn when we talk of these days; think, then, what those endured who, like your grandfather, had been citizens of the proudest nation on earth, which had never known disgrace or defeat, and whose boast it used to be that they bore a flag on which the sun never set! We had heard of generosity in war; we found none; the war was made by us, it was said, and we must take the consequences. London and our only arsenal captured, we were at the mercy of our captors, and right heavily did they tread on our necks.

Need I tell you the rest, of the ransom we had to pay, and the taxes raised to cover it, which keep us paupers to this day? The brutal frankness that announced we must give place to a new naval power, and be made harmless for revenge? The victorious troops living at free quarters, the yoke they put on us made the more galling that their requisitions had a semblance of method and legality? Better have been robbed at first hand by the soldiery themselves, than through our own magistrates made the instruments for extortion. How we lived through the degradation we daily and hourly underwent, I hardly even now understand.

And what was there left to us to live for? Stripped of our colonies; Canada and the West Indies gone to America; Australia forced to separate; India lost for ever, after the English there had all been destroyed, vainly trying to hold the country when cut off from aid by their countrymen; Gibraltar and Malta ceded to the new naval power; Ireland independent and in perpetual anarchy and revolution. When I look at my country as it is now—its trade gone, its factories silent, its harbours empty, a prey to pauperism and decay— when I see all this, and think what Great Britain was in my youth, I ask myself whether I have really a heart or any sense of patriotism that I should have witnessed such degradation and still care to live!

France was different. There, too, they had to eat the bread of tribulation under the yoke of the conqueror! Their fall was hardly more sudden or violent than ours; but war could not take away their rich soil; they had no colonies to lose; their broad lands, which made their wealth, remained to them; and they rose again from the blow. But our people could not be got to see how artificial our prosperity was—that it all rested on foreign trade and financial credit; that the course of trade once turned away from us, even for a time, it might never return; and that our credit once shaken might never be restored.

To hear men talk in those days, you would have thought that Providence had ordained that our government should always borrow at 3 percent, and that trade came to us because we lived in a foggy little island set in a boisterous sea. They could not be got to see that the wealth heaped up on every side was not created in the country, but in India and China, and other parts of the world, and that it would be quite possible for the people who made money by buying and selling the natural treasures of the earth, to go and live in other places, and take their profits with them.

Nor would men believe that there could ever be an end to our coal and iron, or that they would get to be so much dearer than the coal and iron of America that it would no longer be worth while to work them, and that therefore we ought to insure against the loss of our artificial position as the great centre of trade, by making ourselves secure and strong and respected. We thought we were living in a commercial millennium, which must last for a thousand years at least.

After all, the bitterest part of our reflection is that all this misery and decay might have been so easily prevented, and that we brought it about ourselves by our own shortsighted recklessness. There, across the narrow Straits, was the writing on the wall, but we would not choose to read it.

The warnings of the few were drowned in the voice of the multitude. Power was then passing away from the class which had been used to rule, and to face political dangers, and which had brought the nation with honour unsullied through former struggles, into the hands of the lower classes, uneducated, untrained to the use of political rights, and swayed by demagogues; and the few who were wise in their generation were denounced as alarmists, or as aristocrats who sought their own aggrandisement by wasting public money on bloated armaments. The rich were idle and luxurious; the poor grudged the cost of defence. Politics had become a mere bidding for Radical votes, and those who should have led the nation stooped rather to pander to the selfishness of the day, and humoured the popular cry which denounced those who would secure the defence of the nation by enforced arming of its manhood, as interfering with the liberties of the people.

Truly the nation was ripe for a fall; but when I reflect how a little firmness and self-denial, or political courage and foresight, might have averted the disaster, I feel that the judgment must have really been deserved. A nation too selfish to defend its liberty, could not have been fit to retain it. To you, my grandchildren, who are now going to seek a new home in a more prosperous land, let not this bitter lesson be lost upon you in the country of your adoption. For me, I am too old to begin life again in a strange country; and hard and evil as have been my days, it is not much to await in solitude the time which cannot now be far off, when my old bones will be laid to rest in the soil I have loved so well, and whose happiness and honour I have so long survived.